Now it's for always

A Novel

Book 2 in the Prince Edward Island
Love Letters & Legends Trilogy

Jessica Eissfeldt

Now It's For Always: A novel
Jessica Eissfeldt

ISBN: 978-1-989290-01-9

FOR A LIMITED TIME
GET YOUR FREE SWEET ROMANCE HERE!

Get your free copy of the sweet romance *Beside A Moonlit Shore*. Normally, it's $2.99, but this GIFT is yours FREE when you sign up to hear from author Jessica Eissfeldt.

When you sign up, not only will you get this FREE GIFT, but you'll also receive sneak peaks of Jessica's upcoming stories, have the opportunity to win prizes, get exclusive subscriber-only content...and more!

After her sea captain husband dies, schoolteacher Anna Hampton wonders if she'll find the courage to love again...beside a moonlit shore.

Go here to get started:
www.jessicaeissfeldt.com/yourfreegift

FOR A LIMITED TIME

ALSO BY JESSICA EISSFELDT

Sweet Historical Romance:

Sweethearts & Jazz Nights
Dialing Dreams
Shattered Melodies
Fancy Footwork
Unspoken Lyrics
The Sweethearts & Jazz Nights Boxed Set:
The Complete Collection

Love By Moonlight
Beneath A Venetian Moon
Beside A Moonlit Shore
The Love By Moonlight Boxed Set: The
Complete Collection

Sweet Contemporary Romance:

Prince Edward Island Love Letters &
Legends
This Time It's Forever
Now It's For Always
At Last It's True Love

To Prince Edward Island—thank you for
the inspiration.

Chapter One

MAGGIE KILHOUGHERY SHOVED her still-blank sketchpad to the side of her desk and looked down at the flash of gold in her palm—the charm bracelet she'd designed and made herself.

Cobalt-blue grosgrain ribbon had been woven in between heavy links in a half-inch wide gold chain. Seven gold coins—designed to look like Spanish doubloons—dangled along the chain's length beside several other treasure-inspired charms: a tiny treasure chest, a pirate ship, and a spyglass.

Such a little thing, and yet...

Her lips curved upward. And yet...it had been the start of everything. Her heart fluttered. She still couldn't quite believe her bracelet had gotten so much attention.

Attention she should be giving to her follow-up piece. Her stomach knotted.

Maggie glanced at *The New York Times* crossword she had almost solved. Just one more word to go. She chewed on the end of her pencil and ignored the sketchpad and the pile of jewelry supply catalogs that she should be going through. On top of the stack was the latest Courtney Jewelers brochure she'd skimmed earlier today. They'd been around since 1815 and rivalled Tiffany & Co. in prestige and quality.

She bit her lip and neatly penciled in the final crossword answer.

She turned her attention to the crypt-o-quote beneath the crossword and was about to start on it when she heard a tentative knock at her half-open door. She looked up to see Nicky, her assistant.

Nicky adjusted her pencil skirt. "We just hit 500,000 followers on all the social media accounts. On the website, too. And, well, our sales are up. Way up. Musta been that social media campaign of yours, hey?"

Nicky beamed and continued. "Oh, and I've had tons of emails and calls—people are wanting to know what you're going to do next." Nicky paused. "You really inspire me, you know? Even with all those failed pitches to style editors and fashion influencers, you've never given up. And now your bracelet's the hottest thing on the market."

Maggie smiled. "Thanks, Nicky." But guilt surged through Maggie. Nicky didn't know the half of it.

When Maggie had decided to launch her own jewelry line, she'd known she wanted each piece to be based on real treasure.

Just like the Tiffany-designed antique bracelet Zak Stuart, her ex almost-fiancé, had given her for her birthday one year.

But when they'd broken up, he hadn't asked for the bracelet back, so she figured she could keep it. She loved to wear it.

So much so that she'd used the antique bracelet as the inspiration to create her charm bracelet. In fact, she brought the antique piece with her to work regularly as a reminder of the quality, history and workmanship she wanted to put into her own jewelry.

She'd launched her charm bracelet as the first piece in her *Treasured Oceans of Love* series.

Since the antique had directly inspired

her own creation, she'd taken artistic license and used Zak's family story about the antique bracelet in the social media campaign she'd undertaken for her charm bracelet. All without Zak's permission.

Maggie fidgeted with one of her pearl earrings. Half a million followers? She swallowed. "It takes inspiration, yes. But hard work is the other half they don't tell you about in school. Designing something inspired by real treasure was a huge risk."

"Real treasure." A light came into Nicky's eyes. "Wow." She hurried off, oblivious to Maggie's inner turmoil.

Before this bracelet, she'd thought her career was over before it began. There'd been only a smattering of sales. Pretty much no one but her friends and family had ever bought anything she'd designed and made. Major design houses kept rejecting her work. The people at Harry Winston said she shouldn't have even bothered approaching them.

She winced. Zak *really* wouldn't like it if he knew she'd implied he was in any way a treasure hunter or involved with treasure hunting.

Maggie tapped a French-manicured

fingernail against the charm bracelet.

The next piece in the series had to not only be as beautiful as this one but also make a statement. She doodled in the margin of the sketchpad. It was all about risk.

That's why she'd decided to look up female pirates. She wanted to convey female power in overcoming obstacles.

But somehow, Anne Bonny, Mary Read and Grace O'Malley had all taken a back seat in her imagination when she'd discovered Eleanor. Her gaze travelled to the tattered, gray-blue clothbound book on the edge of her desk.

She reached for the book, *Petticoats & Pistols: Legends of Female Pirates in Piracy's Golden Age*, published in the 1940s. Eleanor had been a pirate. So she had to have hoarded some sort of treasure, right?

Maggie flipped to water-stained, yellowed page 88. She'd found the beat-up volume on top of an Art Deco dressing table crammed into the back of a dusty antique shop in Greenwich Village.

He saw coming toward him, through the billowing smoke, a tall silhouette. She wore a tricorn hat and a captain's jacket; its brass

buttons gleamed in the moonlight despite the cloud cover overhead. He nearly dropped the bucket as he fumbled for the hilt of his sword. But the woman in the tricorn hat merely laughed. He could see, as the clouds parted for a moment, her sea-green eyes flash emerald in the starlight. She was the most beautiful woman he'd ever laid eyes on. The flames danced and twisted around her, with her raven-dark hair coiled into a tight braid that formed a crown around her head. A jagged scar marred her left cheek. Though his lungs filled with the burning, acrid smoke, he managed to choke out, "Who are you?" The woman touched a necklace at her throat, diamond and emerald rings flashing on her fingers as she did so. She finally spoke—in a whisper-soft voice that commanded his attention with its sweet chiming sound. "Though my eye color and manner in which I dress my hair give cause for others to call me an emerald queen, my name is Eleanor."

Not a very long legend, as these things went. Which was somewhat strange, come to think. The story read more like a first-hand account. Still.

This was something to latch onto. And the tale made Maggie smile every time she read it.

The problem was, she didn't know enough about this pirate named Eleanor. Maggie needed to find out more. She needed to immerse herself in the history of this woman. Know what it felt like to *be* her. Because the more Maggie found out about Eleanor, the more her jewelry would come to life. For 500,000 people who were expecting another great piece.

Her shoulders tensed. The next design had to be something... phenomenal.

Stunning.

Mysterious.

Romantic.

She crumpled up the piece of sketch paper with the half-drawn doodles and tossed it into the trash with the ten other balled-up pages already there.

She sighed. Picked up a fresh sheet of paper and re-sharpened her pencil. Stared at the blank page.

Maggie looked away from her blank page to the pen-and-ink drawing on the book's facing page. The woman's raven-black hair was braided into a crown.

Some wisps escaped from the tightly woven coif. Strands framed her high cheekbones and highlighted a scar underneath her left eye.

The most arresting feature, however, was not the necklace at Eleanor's throat, but the gleam in Eleanor's eyes, captured by the sketch artist. As if she was daring the viewer to have the courage to seek the truth, to follow her heart.

Maggie shook her head. That was her own artistic imagination filling in the blanks. Who knew if the picture was even an accurate portrait?

The drawing, she noticed, had no artist signature. According to the entry, the portrait was done circa 1698.

Maggie was a designer, not a scholar or a historian. She didn't know anyone she could ask about this pirate. Not any more.

She glanced out the window of her tiny office she'd just started to rent. Now that she was becoming successful, she had to have this office, right? The rosy glow of the setting sun touched the skyscrapers. Off in the distance, if she craned her neck and stood in exactly the right spot, she could *almost* see the Empire State Building.

She uncrossed her arms and the contours of her second-hand white silk Armani suit jacket flowed with her movement.

She picked up the antique jewelry piece beside her charm bracelet and carefully placed the antique back in its original leather pouch. She studied the scuff marks on the leather, the cracked edges. This pouch had to be at least 150 years old, if not more...

Her charm bracelet was this season's must-have. The gold flashed in the fading afternoon light. But all she could think was: what would Zak say?

No, it didn't matter.

But her heart clenched, just the tiniest bit.

Because Zak, after all, was the man she'd fallen in love with all those years ago on Prince Edward Island. And the man who never wanted to see her again.

Because, according to him, the last time she'd seen him—the evening they'd broken up—she'd not only stolen his heart, but also smashed it to bits.

DR. ZAK STUART'S grip tightened on the railing of the boat. He inhaled the scent of salt air as the research vessel bobbed ever so slightly off the shore of Bay Fortune, Prince Edward Island. Calm July day. Perfect conditions for exploring underwater here on the Northumberland Strait.

He rubbed the back of his neck and smothered a yawn. He was still adjusting from the jet lag. That conference in Turkey had been great but it felt good to be back in Canada—even if his research grant deadline now loomed.

He glanced down at his Hublot Oceanographic 4000 divers' watch and frowned. He'd gotten it three years ago to celebrate his success in helping to find Captain William Kidd's ship *Adventure Galley*.

And, he shifted his weight, if he was totally honest with himself, he'd also gotten the watch as a way to ease the pain of Maggie breaking up with him.

The watch had certainly lived up to its craftsmanship and advertising—it'd been a trustworthy companion and never failed him once. His frown deepened. Unlike Maggie. Who'd refused his proposal three years ago.

But their relationship was ancient history now, so why had she come to mind after all this time? He adjusted the elapsed time bezel on the watch's face and took a breath. He had to focus on the dive. They just might find the wreck of *Lady's Revenge* today.

And if they did find it, well, he'd be able to finally prove there was a real ship behind the legendary Ghost Ship of the Northumberland Strait. Some of his colleagues wondered how a scientist like him could chase after something as unscientific-sounding as a ghost ship. But Zak had grown up with the stories. Something inside him longed to prove its existence. Its realness. To connect with that part of what he saw as his Island heritage.

The phantom vessel had sailed these waters for over 200 years, but was first sighted in 1786. Down through the centuries, the ship had been seen over and over. By the young. By the old. By disbelievers and devotees. By his granddad, even. But never by him.

Zak's lips quirked.

No one knew why, or where, the ship had originated. And everyone had different theories about its origins. Some had seen it in Nova Scotia. Others, in New

Brunswick. But most often, it had been sighted off the shores of Prince Edward Island.

Canada Post had featured the ghost ship on one of its Haunted Canada stamps. U-Haul had even painted it on the side of their vans—#130 in their Ventures Across Canada series.

Some people said a ghostly Captain Kidd piloted the doomed vessel to pay for some piratical debt.

Others swore the real story was that a P.E.I. Acadian girl fell in love with a sailor whose ship accidentally caught fire.

But no one knew with absolute surety.

Zak's eyes returned to the horizon just off the starboard side of the vessel he'd secured for the project. Not a cloud in sight. Sunlight glinted off the calm waters of the strait.

A porpoise surfaced and Zak felt himself relax. Always a sign of good luck. Not that he was superstitious. But he could use a little luck.

Even though his mentor, Dr. Woods, was along to help out, this was the first time Zak had led a survey project like this since he'd gotten his PhD three years ago.

Zak sighed and stuffed his hands in the pockets of his tan cargo shorts. He had only four weeks left in his year-long deadline to find the shipwreck. He had to find something soon. No wreck meant no more grant funding for the project.

Suddenly his cell phone rang. It was his agent.

"Zak, you must not be diving for gold bars yet since you answered your phone."

"Just about to get into my dry suit." He laughed. "But this isn't a treasure ship. It's a ghost ship. Sure, I mean, some of the local lore says Kidd had something to do with the vessel. But his name pops up all the time when you're talking about this type of thing. The treasure I'm seeking is the shipwreck itself."

"Sure, sure. I bet all nautical archaeologists say that," his agent joked. "Well, I won't keep you, but I just wanted to give you some good news. The acquisitions team at Simon & Schuster loved the on-spec pitch. They were especially intrigued by the ghost ship."

Zak's heart beat a little faster. If he could publish his book, *Legendary Shipwrecks of the North Atlantic: Real Facts*

Behind the Fiction, it would solve every-thing.

Well, maybe that was a stretch. But publishing about this find would help open doors to more money to continue the project. Because, once he found the ship, he'd need more funds to actually excavate it. A big-name publisher would mean excellent exposure, too.

If he could prove that the phantom ship had existed as a real vessel, he'd have the scientific answers to a legend over 200 years old.

"Really?" Zak cleared his throat and hoped that the excitement wasn't too evident in his voice. He had to remain professional.

"What you're doing, it's like a real life Clive Cussler novel."

Zak chewed his lip. He'd conjectured the latitude and longitude from the travel journal of explorer and fur trader Henry Davies. But what if he didn't find the wreck?

"You find that wreck, Zak, and the publisher's willing to not only sign you, but also give you a big advance. Five figures."

Zak scrubbed a hand across his jawline.

"You've submitted all the other chapters on all the other shipwrecks. When can you have that last chapter on the ghost ship to me so I can pass it along?"

"I'll have it to you as soon as I can. I have a good feeling about things today. Once we find the ship, I can write up that final chapter."

"Sounds good. Talk soon," his agent said.

Zak ended the call and took a big breath. Five figures. Zak ruffled his hair with a free hand and shifted his weight. The university would get a chunk of that amount, but he'd get a pretty big piece of it, too, which he could then use to help with the project's future expenses.

Memorial University provided a modest amount but they weren't set up to handle really big projects. And this was a pretty big project.

But he'd gotten lucky. The project was deemed not only culturally exciting but also significant historically, so he'd been given a grant and the go-ahead for the year-long project.

Which meant, if they actually found the wreck, it would be worthy of mounting a full-scale excavation and all the funding that came with it.

If they didn't... He winced. It'd be hard to get future funding and he'd lose professional credibility, too.

Not only that, while he'd grown up, he'd seen his father, and his grandfather, fail time and again at what they held so dear. So, deep down, he felt he owed it to his family to succeed with this. He tightened his jaw. He wasn't going to give up on something that he'd believed for so long was real.

He'd taken a chance, persuaded every-one on the committee that this shipwreck was not only real but also could be found.

Which was pretty miraculous, given that, according to his research, *Lady's Revenge* had gone down after being set ablaze.

Which meant it would've been in piec-es as it sank. As a result, there might be little left to find on the sea floor now.

"Dr. Stuart?" His graduate assistant approached. "The side-scan sonar's completed its search of this section of the sea floor."

"Great, let's take a look."

They headed to the cabin, where the three other members of Zak's team were assembled. Zak took a seat at the main computer next to the other scanning equipment.

"The sonar's scanned this area for significant bumps or shadows." The assistant pointed to the computer screen. "It found four potential places we can dive."

"Well, this is a morale boost." Zak studied the screen. "Let's drop buoys at each of those four spots the sonar picked up and see what we can find." He paused and addressed everyone. "But remember, because of the red silt and clay that make up the strait bottom, we have to expect some sinking, especially in shallow waters like these with a bit of turbulence. So let's not expect to go down and see something immediately just lying on the sea floor. Evidence of the ship will at least be partially buried."

The others nodded.

A few minutes later, Zak zipped up his dry suit and adjusted his goggles. He glanced over at Dr. Woods, his dive partner. If they didn't find anything in this section of sea floor at the first target, they would've wasted another few days of their rapidly dwindling four-week period.

And they'd have to move the boat and send down the sonar again to scan a new section of the larger search area.

He stepped off the back of the boat.

MAGGIE GLANCED AT the clock. Almost time to go. Just then, the phone on her desk rang.

"Maggie Kilhoughery speaking. How can I help you?"

"Maggie, I'm with the *Sun*. Just a few quick questions. To confirm, your site just hit half a million followers. And your sales are through the roof. Tell me, how did you do it, coming out of nowhere like that? What's the secret behind your success?"

Maggie's stomach churned. "Yes, I can confirm we've hit half a million followers and nearly double that in sales. It's great." She paused. "Sorry, but I'm not doing any interviews at the moment."

"Oh, come on, now, Maggie. Don't be coy. Everyone wants to know the real story."

Maggie swallowed. "Everyone?"

The reporter laughed. "All of your fans."

The real story... Memory washed over Maggie.

"Back in the 1880s, my great-great grandfather Samuel Stuart commissioned Charles Lewis Tiffany to design this bracelet as a gift for his new bride." Zak said, as he held out the gold bracelet. It caught the moonlight. *"And now I want you to have it."*

Maggie's eyes widened. "But Zak, why are you giving this to me? You don't even like treasure hunting."

Zak grinned. "You're right. I don't." He stroked her cheek. "But I want you to have this piece of my family history, this piece of me... so you can remember me even when I'm not here."

They gazed at each other for a silent moment. Maggie touched a fingertip to the gold coin that dangled from the delicate chain. "Since treasure hunting runs in your family, Samuel must've had this coin, then?"

"Yep," Zak said. "You remember I told you he'd been running around looking for that lost treasure? Well, his friend named Robert Morriss had gotten it from a treasure

hunter named Thomas Jefferson Beale. But Morriss didn't have time to go off treasure hunting, so he gave Samuel the coin."

Then Zak continued. "Tiffany made this bracelet. He attached that single gold doubloon to this delicate chain that he hand-etched with a design of flowers and vines." Zak tucked a loose strand of hair behind her ear. "The coin was rumored to be from Kidd's hoard."

Maggie looked down at the bracelet that Zak had unclasped.

"I know how much you love all these romantic stories connected to lost treasure. So," Zak whispered, "that's why I'm giving it to you." He fastened the gold chain around her wrist. "Happy birthday."

"Oh, Zak," Maggie said, voice husky.

Maggie shook off the memory. "I'm not in a position to answer any more questions right now. I'm sorry."

"Are you sure about that?"

Maggie's hand clenched around the phone. "Yes."

"Just five minutes."

"No," Maggie said.

"Well, I'm sure I'll find out one way or the other."

"I'm sorry but I'm not doing any interviews right now. Good bye." She hung up then grimaced. Zak would truly hate her forever if she let the press find out it was *his* family story behind that social media campaign.

Why did she care what Zak thought of her any more? It'd been three years...

Besides, he was off in Turkey on some nautical archaeological summit, last she'd heard. He'd be more inclined to read an issue of *Archaeology* than *Vogue* or *Vanity Fair*—both of which had mentioned her bracelet on their own social media platforms.

Besides, she didn't care what anyone thought of her. She hadn't gotten this far by being nice.

She got up and put the small leather pouch into her sample-sale red leather Hermes bag, slung the purse over her shoulder, locked her office door, and headed home to her rented brownstone.

Her cell phone buzzed. She glanced at the text from Nicky. *You just missed a call from Courtney.* Maggie replied: *Did you get a last name?* A second later, her phone buzzed again. *Uh, it was Courtney Jewelers.*

THE BLUE WATERS of the Northumberland Strait closed over Zak. The water was clear and warm. P.E.I. had the warmest water north of the Carolinas because of the Gulf currents that flowed up here.

As Zak's senses adjusted to the watery environment, he focused on the sea floor.

Sand and silt. Nothing else.

He swam further. Watched the fluorescent-yellow swim fins of his dive partner move off to the side.

Lobsters and crabs scuttled around clumps of mermaid's purse, yellow-green seaweed and tufts of sea grass.

His eyes scanned the sea floor. Still nothing but sand and silt.

His jaw tightened. There had to be something here. The sonar had picked it up.

He glanced up from his close study of the sea bed. A dark shape loomed in front of him. His heart pounded. This must have been what the sonar picked up. As he stretched out a hand, he realized it was nothing more than solid sandstone.

Technology was great. But sometimes

it couldn't tell the difference between wreck-shaped rocks and rock-shaped wrecks.

They'd have to search elsewhere. He gestured to his dive partner and they headed to the surface.

But hours later, when Zak clambered up onto the deck for the fourth time without results, he fought down the bitter disappointment that clawed at the back of his throat.

Sunset streaked the water pink. Looked like tomorrow they'd have to move the boat and send down the sonar again to scan a new section of the larger search area, after all.

He'd triple-checked everything.

But maybe he'd miscalculated the margin of error he'd set for the ocean currents. Or the tides. Or the weight of whatever cargo might've been in the hold of the wreck.

Or maybe so much silt covered the ship on the sea floor that the equipment was thrown off. Hell, it could even be that centuries of sea creatures had eaten away the entire thing...

He gave a frustrated sigh.

But that was the risk he'd taken, he supposed, when he'd decided to hunt for this thing. He wasn't going to give up the search. Especially not now. But he did have to head in for the night.

He stripped out of his dry suit and grabbed his cargo shorts and put them on. Then he reached for his favorite T-shirt, the one with the logo of Memorial University of Newfoundland Sea-Hawks.

Maggie had always hated this shirt. Too old and holey, she'd said. She had always been pretty opinionated. He tugged the shirt on over his head. As the familiar soft cotton fabric brushed his bare skin and settled around him, he felt a sense of longing wash through him.

Maggie.

That's why he kept this shirt, if he was completely honest with himself. Because it reminded him of her. And because it reminded him that at least he hadn't failed at his career... yet.

He'd gotten his undergrad at UPEI. Then he'd gotten his master's in archaeology from Memorial University in Newfoundland and his doctorate from Texas A & M in nautical archaeology. After he'd graduated at the top of his class, he'd snagged a prime position back at Memorial in nautical archaeology. If only he could bring the sense of comfort and familiarity from his work into his personal life.

He wished for a second that things had worked out between him and Maggie. Then shoved that thought forcefully away as he stepped sockless into his Top-Sider boat shoes.

Zak gestured to two of his other team members—Dr. Woods had decided to stay on the water a bit longer—and headed over to the dinghy that would take the three of them to shore.

No. She'd betrayed his trust in her.

His mouth tightened as he piloted the dinghy. He'd trusted her—twice with his heart and once with his heirloom. She'd never given that damn bracelet back, either.

His grip tightened on the wheel. That was a piece of his family's history she'd stolen. She'd probably sold it so she could buy a new pair of designer heels.

He frowned. Seems that he'd had more failures than successes. His almost-engagement to Maggie. And now, his

inability—yet again—to find the phantom ship.

He swore under his breath. Thinking like this wasn't going to get him anywhere. He took a breath. He had to remain positive.

But a trickle of weariness slipped into his system anyway. The dinghy nudged up against the pier. How many more times was he going to be wrong?

Zak payed out the lines. This was the best damn chance they'd had to find the wreck, what with Davies' journal practically stating where the ship had caught fire.

Well, he'd just have to try harder. He stepped onto the pier and used two half-hitches to make fast the dinghy to the moorings.

After his two other team members had stepped ashore, Zak double-checked that the knots were tight.

"Dr. Stuart," Zak's assistant said, "once we finish these errands, we'll take the dinghy back out to pick up Dr. Woods."

Zak nodded then headed toward his navy blue four-door Dodge pickup truck.

He got in and turned the key. The engine came to life with a rumble and the radio came on too. He turned up the volume on the CBC news as he drove down Fortune Wharf North Road.

"—storms start earlier than ever. Though Prince Edward Island usually only gets tropical storms and not full-fledged hurricanes, experts predict that this season is going to have hurricanes sweeping through the province, so Islanders need to be extra-prepared."

Zak pursed his lips as he turned on to Route 310. Forecasting the intensity of storms could be a bit tricky, he knew from experience. Because where the storms went depended on the weather of the day, not just on what meteorologists said.

He flicked the channels until he found the local pop station, Ocean 100, and followed Route 310 back along the bay.

Supposedly, Bay Fortune had been originally called that because Captain Kidd had buried a fortune somewhere around the area.

Zak had never believed it. There were too many long hard winters with too little for Islanders to do other than entertain themselves with lore like that. His frown deepened. Tales that only encouraged fortune hunters like his great-grandfather, James P. Stuart.

Zak shook that thought away and rolled down his window.

Pine trees flashed by. He took a deep breath of the pine-scented air that still held the tang of salt and turned on to Howe Point Road.

Though he was originally from the north shore of the island—Dalvay by the Sea, up Covehead way—he'd rented a rambling old Victorian house near Bay Fortune for the summer while he worked on the project. He pulled into the drive and went up to the house.

After he grabbed the latest edition of Charlottetown's local paper, *The Guardian,* off the porch, he ate a quick dinner of cold pasta. Then he headed over to the box of research books he'd brought with him and aimlessly began to go through the pile.

He glanced at the small leather-bound book that should, he mused, actually be in a museum instead of in his possession. Yet Davies' journal, which sat in its own container, was the only solid piece of evidence he had.

Because the journal mentioned a real

ship that not only matched the phantom vessel's description but also went down in flames—87 years before the first alleged ghost ship sighting.

But Zak didn't pick up the journal. Instead, his fingers closed around a cheap pasteboard kids' book titled *Secret Codes, Secret Ciphers.* Despite himself, a small smile flicked across his face. He wouldn't hear the end of it if his colleagues knew he kept this around. He picked up the familiar volume and flipped to the flyleaf. *For Zak, on your eighth birthday. Happy treasure hunting, son! Love, Granddad*

Zak turned to battered, dog-eared page 58 without thinking. His eyes scanned the familiar lines.

The Beale Papers: Hoax or Fact?

Thomas Jefferson Beale stayed for several months at the Washington Hotel located in Lynchburg, Virginia, back in 1822. The innkeeper, Robert Morriss, didn't know it at the time but Beale was on the trail of a treasure.

Before Beale left, he gave Morriss a locked box for safekeeping. Beale

told Morriss that if he didn't return in ten years, Morriss should open the locked iron box and read the enciphered information inside.

Beale never returned. And, though Beale had promised to send a cipher key to Morriss so he could decipher the box's contents, that didn't show up either.

Morriss was left with a dilemma. Should he wait for Beale or open the box? But after more than 20 years, Morriss decided to open the box.

Inside, Morriss found a note—written by Beale—that was wrapped around a single Spanish doubloon. But there were also three other pages there, enciphered in some sort of number code. In the note, Beale explained that he and his partners had found a vast treasure in New Mexico that they'd dug up and carted back to Virginia.

Once back in Virginia, one of Beale's partners, John MacDonald, revealed that, according to his grandfather, Nicholas MacDonald, a portion of the treasure they'd found, specifically a collection of Spanish gold doubloons, had belonged to Captain Kidd. Beale's note went on to say he'd enclosed a single coin, now in Morriss's possession, as proof of this.

Beale also mentioned that John had hinted even more treasure was to be found. But John didn't know any more about it. John said his only clue came from his grandfather Nicholas, one of Kidd's crewmen, who had confessed on his deathbed that some treasure was hidden on "an island east of Boston."

Morriss couldn't decipher the three pages and had no time for treasure hunting. So, in 1862 Morriss passed those pages—and the single coin—on to a friend. That friend would become the anonymous author of the Beale Papers. The Beale Papers, published as a twenty-three page pamphlet in 1885, contained the three enciphered pages and the story about the treasure.

Zak traced a finger along the crude childish printing that spelled out his great-great grandfather's name: Samuel Stuart.

Zak had scrawled the name in blue ballpoint pen above and across the words 'anonymous author of the Beale Papers.' He had such faith in Granddad's stories when he was a kid. When he was in grade school, he daydreamed all the time about how he'd discover piles of gold coins under every tree.

Zak shut the book, shook his head and sighed.

Samuel Stuart wrote the Beale Papers, and Zak's dad also knew that Beale and MacDonald claimed more of Kidd's treasure was out there. So Zak's father concluded that the crewman's deathbed confession meant he'd be able to find more of Kidd's treasure on P.E.I.

But Dad had paid for treasure hunting with his life. Just like Samuel had.

Thanks to a bad accident at a dig site, Dad had died just before Zak went into his last year of high school. Zak's lips compressed into a line and he put away the children's book.

Dad's death was when and why Zak

had vowed to never become a treasure hunter.

Zak turned his attention back to his research. After he slipped on white cotton preservation gloves, he picked up the slim leather-bound travel journal. Then he sat down at the kitchen table.

He placed the book on a clean kitchen towel and flicked on the table lamp he'd moved for the purpose.

There had to be something else in here that he'd missed the first time. The question was, what?

MAGGIE STOPPED ON the sidewalk and stared at her phone. Courtney Jewelers? She blinked. Straightened her shoulders. She'd call the jewelry company back first thing tomorrow morning.

She opened the elegant wrought iron gate and unlocked the door of the convert-ed brownstone. She pushed open the door to what once had been a grand foyer but was now the entry to her small studio apartment.

The evening light caught the leaded

cut-glass fanlight and sent a shimmer of rainbows onto the worn red and blue Oriental runner in the hall.

Maggie smiled as she inhaled the scent of vanilla and oleander from her favourite Crate & Barrel candle. It sat on the reproduction Louis XVI hall table she'd found at a rummage sale.

She stepped out of her black faux Gucci pumps and sighed in relief as she rotated her ankles and stretched her toes. She hung up her purse in the hall closet. She put her house keys and the leather pouch that contained the antique bracelet onto the side table. She'd have to put the bracelet away in the bedroom safe later this evening.

A slight scuffling sound on polished hardwood made her grin. Pierniki, her big Maine Coon cat, just over a year old, trotted up to her.

He wound himself around her ankles. His loud purr rumbled a soft vibration against her legs.

She leaned down and stroked his head, and his bright yellow eyes watched her. She smiled. Pierniki still thought he was a kitten. He loved to get into mischief.

"All right there, big boy. Come on, let's look in the kitchen cabinet. I never feed you at all, now, do I?" she teased.

Pierniki just blinked then turned and trotted toward the kitchen counter.

Maggie laughed ruefully to herself. What was this saying about her social life, that she enjoyed talking to her cat sometimes more than her own friends?

Never mind that Pierniki was the only male companionship she'd entertained in longer than she cared to remember.

Maggie made a face at her mopey thoughts then padded barefoot to the kitchen, where she placed a portion of Fancy Feast into Pierniki's dish. She crouched down and petted him while he ate.

"How about it, Pier? Do you think I should stop making up fantasy men in my head? Get out there more and go on some dates?"

Pierniki just kept eating.

"Well, you're right." She sighed as she blinked back sudden tears. "I guess I'm just a little..." she cleared her throat. "Some companionship would be nice."

Maggie rubbed the cat behind his ears.

She tucked a strand of her own shoulder-length dark hair behind her ear and then grabbed the leftover Mexican takeout from last night out of the fridge. She heated it up in the microwave, rummaged around for a fork in the silverware drawer and then took the food and settled onto the creamy white leather sofa. She pulled a pale blue cashmere throw over her. Then she took a few bites of the leftovers with the fork she wielded.

See? She was just fine by herself. Maybe it didn't matter that she hadn't seriously dated anyone since Zak.

She winced. And that was three years ago. Not that she hadn't gone on dates since then. She had. They'd just all been first dates that had headed nowhere.

Her phone buzzed. She glanced at the text from her friend Sarah. *Hey! The girls are going to that new place that just opened in Tribeca. Join us for a drink?*

Thanks for the offer, Maggie texted back, *but I just need some alone time tonight. Feel like I've been running a million miles an hour for the last month. Maybe next week?*

But before she could put the phone aside, it dinged with another incoming message along with a photo. *Having a great time with Nathan in Ireland!* Maggie smiled at the picture of her friend Ruby with her new husband Nathan. Married life seemed to suit Ruby. Maggie sent a smile emoticon back and a note that said they'd have to chat when Ruby got back from her honeymoon.

Maggie laid the phone down beside her as her thoughts went back to her work. If she was honest with herself, a lot of the stress was from her least favorite part of the business—overseeing the day-to-day administrative details. Going in to the office. She just wanted to create jewelry and didn't want to have to worry about spreadsheets and inventory numbers and staff... But, she supposed, that was part of the deal, wasn't it?

She frowned and her thoughts drifted back to Zak. Why did she always use him as the yardstick for any other man she came into contact with? It wasn't fair to those other men, or to him, or to herself.

Besides all that, it wasn't healthy. That wasn't what she needed or wanted in her life—to be hung up on someone with whom things had long since finished.

No. She wasn't hung up on Zak. She just hadn't found anyone else as compatible as she'd felt, thought, *known*, they'd been. She shook her head. Dislodged the negative thought spiral. She was happy. Really. She was doing what she loved. Had great friends. Loved this city. She took another bite of burrito.

Was she a fraud? After all, she'd basically stolen the story of the bracelet. She shifted on the couch cushions. But it was a story that needed to be told. And obviously it had resonated with her target audience. Even if she hadn't told Zak she'd "borrowed" his family story for the social media campaign.

If that ever got out... everything she'd worked so hard for would disappear. And what a relief that would be.

Maggie sat up straight at the thought. No. She hadn't meant that.

She gave new life to priceless, historic objects—pieces that would otherwise molder in museum back rooms—and used them as inspiration for her art. That was *not* fraud.

To pass those feelings of freedom and enjoyment to her customers, that was her true passion in life. It gave the everyday woman a chance to have a little piece of treasure for herself.

She shook her head. Remembered the excitement she'd felt when Zak had first given her the bracelet. She sighed. Had she made the right choice to refuse Zak's proposal? She'd kept the bracelet because it reminded her of Zak, of their time together, of their connection. Over the years, she'd thought about sending the bracelet back to him. But she somehow couldn't quite bring herself to do it. That would've been like trying to send him back a piece of her own heart—

A loud clunk from the hallway broke into her revere. The sound of glass shattering made her leap up from the couch and head toward the foyer. Her heart pounded.

She flicked on the hall light and made herself walk carefully down the short hall in the direction of the sound. No one had broken the front door open. There was nothing out of place—

The side table.

The unlit Crate & Barrel candle had fallen. The crystal candle holder she'd

placed the candle in had also fallen to the floor and shattered into a million sparkling shards. She noticed the strands of cat hair amongst the mess.

The corners of her lips tugged up into a smile. Pierniki liked to keep her on her toes. In this case, literally.

She grabbed the broom and dustpan out of the hall closet and started to sweep up the mess. As she crouched down with the dustpan, she spotted the leather pouch that contained the antique bracelet.

As she reached under the table for the pouch, she noticed the tooth marks along the edge of the leather. Pierniki thought everything was a toy.

As she closed her fingers around the ancient pouch, the bracelet fell out the bottom. The cat must have chewed all the way through the stitching. Crap.

At least the bracelet hadn't been damaged. Unlike her modern charm bracelet, this antique had a very simple design: a single Spanish doubloon on a delicate one-fourth inch gold chain.

She put the bracelet back on the side table but the recent mauling was too much for the ancient pouch's stitching. The whole piece of leather fell apart at its seams.

Maggie winced. Something else Zak wouldn't like if he knew about it. When he'd given her the bracelet, it'd been inside that leather pouch.

Zak had told her that originally, the pouch had contained only the single gold doubloon. Then somewhere along the line, the coin had been fastened to the chain to make the bracelet.

She placed the pouch, now a flat rectangle, onto the side table and then turned on the table lamp. She'd have to put it into a plastic bag to protect it.

As she returned to the side table with a Ziploc baggie, a dark blot on the exposed leather interior caught her eye. Must be a stain from the leather dye—

But no. She looked again. It was—she frowned—not an ink stain. She peered closer. It was whole sentences. She held her breath as she read it.

Emerald queen of the North Atlantic deep,
Jewelled heart of stone that does not sleep.
An earl, a Speaker; a Captain's unheard plea.
Twenty-three cryptic pages,
Nearly All lost to a treasure's ravages.

Maggie felt goose bumps rise on her arms, and the sudden brush of soft fur against her legs made her startle.

She glanced down at her cat, who looked up at her with his round golden eyes. Pierniki blinked and she scratched him under the chin.

Where had this come from? Zak hadn't mentioned anything about this...verse?...poem? in the story he'd told her about the bracelet.

She bit her lip as guilt nudged at her. She sighed. For a second, she wished she could just call him up and ask...

The lines almost seemed—she shook her head—like a riddle. But that was impossible. That sort of thing only happened in novels. Didn't it?

ZAK GAVE A huff of irritation. Even if he continued to stare down at the leather-bound book, it wasn't going to make any new information suddenly appear. He needed some fresh air.

He headed out to his pickup. Crickets chirped.

A drive would clear his head. Maybe give him some ideas for what damn step to take next now that he'd run into yet another dead end.

With his mind on autopilot, he took a left out of the driveway and headed to the TransCanada.

After driving for about forty minutes, he found himself approaching the capital city of Charlottetown.

Instead of heading downtown and stopping for a drink at the Churchill Arms on Queen Street like he might've usually done, he kept going along Capital Drive.

On impulse, he took the roundabout toward Argyle Shores and drove through the twilight.

God. He hadn't been out this way in years... Not since he and Maggie had been together.

He drove in silence for awhile before he flicked on the radio to Ocean 100. Tapped his fingers against the steering wheel to the latest pop hit.

He'd never admit to any of his buddies but he actually liked pop music. He cranked up the volume, cranked down the window and began to sing along.

A little while later, the beam from his headlights cut across the grove of rather windblown pines and his tires crunched on the gravel of the parking lot at Argyle Shores Provincial Park.

He got out and took a deep breath. The wind picked up and buffeted his hair. He headed across the grass. Felt the wind blow harder against him the closer he got to the cliff's edge. Moonlight spread across the Northumberland Strait.

A bit of chop out there tonight, he noticed. He headed for the wooden stairs that hugged the craggy cliff face. The stairs creaked as he descended. Tide was out.

After he reached the bottom step, his scuffed up, brown leather Wolverine work boots crunched slightly on the reddish sand and rocks. He took another deep breath. Out here, he could actually breathe. Could actually feel alive again. He tilted his head back and looked up.

A million pin-pricks of light winked back at him.

Yes. Out here, he could actually feel free from career pressures. The wind picked up again, and he welcomed the salt spray of the incoming waves.

Freedom to explore and have adventures.

That was all he really wanted.

Maggie hadn't understood that. It was such an integral part of who he was.

He absently picked up a small piece of sandstone that had flaked off the cliff face. He flicked his wrist. The stone skipped six or eight times across the water before it sank beneath the surface.

He reached down and picked up another sandy stone. The toes of his boots scuffled against the damp seaweed and greenish lichen that covered the sandstone rocks.

He walked a bit farther. His shoes squelched on the damp sand. But he didn't care.

That freedom to have adventures was why he needed to explore. Where he got the urge to dive. Why he'd become a nautical archaeologist in the first place.

Because there in the peace and silence of the deep, he could get in touch with a deeper part of himself. Explore the connection to the history left behind on the sea floor...

He noticed the wind had brought in

some clouds and the moonlight had begun to wane. As his eyes followed the scuttle and rush of the clouds, a shiver climbed up his spine. He rubbed his arms against goosebumps and shoved his hands deeper into his jeans pockets, but the slight chill remained.

He scanned the horizon and wondered whether he should grab his hoodie from the truck. But then his eyes caught a flicker of light on the far, far horizon, out in the darkest part of the strait.

As he watched, the flicker of light seemed to get bigger and brighter. It appeared simultaneously to move toward him yet pull away.

His breath caught in his throat and he swallowed hard and blinked rapidly.

But the light remained.

In fact, it had quadrupled in size and substance in the few moments he'd watched it. And it began to head, he now realized, as the slight chill continued to persist, straight toward him. It was now no longer just a flicker of pale yellow light. It was now a distinct bright orange. The same bright orange he knew to be that of fire.

Flames, to be more precise.

They licked at the darkness, at the blackness, as if it were paper. The orange glow grew bigger. And closer. And bigger still. Until he could see the flames had taken on a distinct shape. A certain outline. One that Islanders the whole province over knew. That of a ship.

A burning ship.

Zak couldn't move even if he wanted to. The sight froze him to the spot as the flames licked higher and higher still.

The shape drew even closer, so that now, he could see flames consume the yardarm, the keel and the bow of a four-masted tall ship.

Over the rush of the surf and the howl of the wind, he heard the crackle of the fire as it continued to burn, bright and hot.

He held his breath.

He could even hear the shouted orders, the muffled thuds and the coarse oaths, as the crew fought for not only their lives but also for their ship. Water splashed as some sailors jumped overboard.

Another splash sounded, and his attention went to a small rowboat that came around the bow of the burning ship.

He cocked his head. He hadn't heard

that happen in any of the reports he'd read for his research. The shouts of the sailors and crackle of the flames grew louder.

His fingers closed reflexively around his cell phone. But he knew that a call would do no good.

That this particular crew, and this particular ship, could not, would not, be saved.

Because this—he blinked quickly and his heart pounded even as he watched the last of the sails become engulfed in flame, and the shouts of the crew turn to screams—was an apparition.

"The ghost ship," Zak whispered. He'd spent his career wondering if he'd ever see it.

Until now.

Chapter Two

WEDNESDAY MORNING, MAGGIE chewed on a cuticle for a second as she stared at the phone on her desk. But she pushed aside the fragments of guilt along with the charm bracelet, and picked up the receiver to call back Courtney Jewelers.

"This is Maggie Kilhoughery. What can I do for you?"

"Well, Maggie," the woman on the other end of the line said, "My name is Jia Rathod. I'm from Courtney Jewelers."

Maggie felt her palms begin to sweat.

"To get straight to the point, Maggie, Courtney Jewelers wants your talent."

"Oh?" Maggie swallowed.

"This charm bracelet you've designed has been selling like crazy on your website—you've had such big numbers that we couldn't help but notice. We keep an eye out for up and coming designers like

you."

Maggie's pulse pounded.

"We'd like you to design a new piece for us." A pause. "We especially loved the story behind the bracelet."

Maggie's stomach clenched.

But the woman continued. "Because of that social media campaign you did, everyone wants to feel like they're part of the romance. Part of the history. Part of the legend. And your bracelet, thanks not only to the exquisite design, but also to the story behind it, does exactly that. So, we want your next piece to have just as compelling of a story behind it."

Maggie felt her mouth go dry. "Well, I know of a certain female pirate who has a very compelling story." She winced. If she could find anything else out about her, that is.

"Great. If things go well, we'd like to pick up your whole *Treasured Oceans of Love* line."

"That'd be—" Maggie cleared her throat "—fantastic." She chuckled. "Er, I mean, I'd be open to that possibility."

"Wonderful," the woman said. "We need the preliminary drawings for this new piece by the end of next week."

"The end of...next week?" Maggie echoed. Today was Wednesday. Her stomach dipped. That gave her only nine days.

"Exactly," the woman confirmed. "If things go well, we'll be in touch again to set up a meeting and draw up the contract and all the other paperwork."

"Okay," Maggie said. "Sounds great." She hung up the phone.

Oh God. What if she couldn't come up with anything? What if she didn't have any more good ideas? What if that bracelet was her only success—No. She shook her head. She'd think of something. She just needed to expand on an idea.

That meant more research. And more research meant help. Yes. That was the answer. She felt the panic begin to ease. She didn't have to do this alone.

She picked up the tattered blue hardcover, got up from her desk and went over to Nicky's workspace. "I need you to find out everything and anything you can about this woman named Eleanor." She handed Nicky the book. "It's for the next piece in the line."

"Okay." Nicky scribbled down notes.

"I'll look for whatever I can find associated with her."

"I haven't found much about her online, so you may need to call people. Use this book as a place to start. Page 88 has some about her. Then look through libraries, that sort of thing. I need to find out as much as possible so I can figure out where I'm coming from with this next design. And if you can, set up a few meetings for me to talk with any experts you may find. By Friday, please."

This was legitimate research. It might take a bit more time away from her actual sketching. But it would be worth it when the design was perfect.

And it *had* to be perfect. This was for Courtney Jewelers, after all.

"Experts." Nicky nodded. Scribbled more notes. "I'll dig up whoever I can."

EARLY FRIDAY AFTERNOON, Maggie sat at her desk, a clean piece of sketch paper in front of her. But her mind was as blank as the page.

When the knock sounded at her door,

she welcomed the distraction. "Nicky. Find anything?"

"I spent a lot of time at the library and on the phone yesterday and this morning. All I found was this one reference in *From Maids to Matriarchs: Unconventional Women Through the Ages.* Got it in a second-hand bookstore in Brooklyn." Nicky handed Maggie a photocopied page.

Eleanor Webster: (c.1660-?) An American woman, born about 1660 near what is now Plymouth, Massachusetts, Eleanor was the daughter of a successful merchant. While from a prominent Puritan family and relatively well off, she was nonetheless accused of witchcraft. She narrowly escaped being burned at the stake. Soon after, she stole one of her father's merchant ships and took to the high seas. Then she sailed for the East Indies, intent to captain her own fleet. What happened to her after that, is, however, lost to history. Scholars debate whether she was a real person or simply a fictional character.

"Great job, Nicky. Thanks so much. You deserve a promotion!"

Nicky laughed. "Don't worry, I won't hold you to that. Oh, and I finally tracked down an expert—sort of. His assistant said he and his research team are working on some shipwreck project in the North Atlantic in the era you're interested in. His assistant also said this guy wasn't exactly an expert on Eleanor but that he had heard of her and had some primary sources, apparently, that talk about her."

"Thanks so much, Nicky. Go ahead and set up a meeting with him."

"I thought you might say that, so I've already done it. He's okayed it. His assistant said you could even come on board, ask questions, observe for awhile if you like. Maybe for an afternoon or even a full day."

"Oh?" Well, the more in-depth, the better. She needed all the inspiration she could get. If spending some time out on a boat would help, she'd do it. "Great. Go ahead and set that up for me, please. You can take care of all the details. Where is it?"

"On Prince Edward Island."

Maggie bit her lip and fidgeted with a button on her blue pinstripe blouse. She hadn't been back there in... three years.

"They'll be ready to meet you Sunday at 7 a.m."

"Okay. I guess I can wrap things up on the island in a day or two, then come back here and actually create the piece."

"Didn't you grow up on Prince Edward Island?"

Maggie nodded. But she, her parents and her siblings now all lived off-island.

"Well that'll be nice for you to be back there for a bit," Nicky said as she turned to go. "When should I book your flight for?"

What Nicky didn't know was that P.E.I. was where she and Zak had fallen in love in high school then called it quits. Where she and Zak had *almost* gotten engaged. And the one place she hoped she'd never have to go back to.

"As soon as possible. Oh, and Nicky? I didn't catch a name. Who's the expert I'll be working with?"

"Dr. Zak Stuart."

ZAK, IN A pair of worn blue jeans and a faded maroon Texas Aggies T-shirt, opened the sliding door to the back patio Friday evening. He stepped out into the golden light, a mug of his usual steaming Earl Grey in hand.

The ship sighting flashed through his mind again. That rowboat wasn't in any of the other hundreds of accounts he'd studied—only in Davies' journal.

He took a sip of tea. But maybe he should check again.

He headed back inside and took a seat on the beat-up suede couch. He reached for the thick binder on the side table.

He propped his bare feet up on the brown leather ottoman and then began to flip through the pages.

Always the same thing, though. People described a tall ship with three or four masts.

Sometimes it was already burning when they saw it. Other times, it burst into flames as they watched.

He turned another page but he knew the material so well that he didn't have to really read it. Sightings were mostly at night. Or dusk. And usually between

September and November. Though some had seen it in the summer months.

He rubbed his temples. Everyone saw it in different places. Along the South Shore. The western side of the island. The sand dunes along the North Shore.

Which essentially meant the wreck could be anywhere. He put aside the binder. Picked up his cotton gloves beside the slim volume written by Davies.

That's why he'd been so excited to find Davies' journal last month before he'd headed to Turkey for the summit.

He'd found the leather-bound book at an estate sale near Georgetown, P.E.I.

Some lobster fisherman's great-great grandmother had found it, the old lady had said. It had been in the family ever since.

Until they'd sold it at the estate sale, anyway.

He put on the gloves and carefully opened the cracked leather volume.

He paged through it until he found the entry that mentioned Davies' campsite—the location Zak conjectured the wreck to be near.

2 July 1701

My journey with the Hudson's Bay Company ends at last. Have set up camp and await my Beloved.

But my worry grows great, as here, along the mouth of Bay Fortune, Eleanor assured me she would dock. Though neither she nor Lady's Revenge have shown themselves to be in evidence. I fear Kidd's Quartermaster may be the cause.

The entry ended abruptly. Zak turned the abnormally thick page. The next few pages had only faded ink sketches of Mi'kmaq dwellings and various wildlife. Notes about paddle routes dotted the margins alongside tallies of beaver and fox pelts.

Zak found the next entry. The penmanship was unsteady and the ink marred in several places.

15 July 1701

No moon tonight. An ill omen, mayhap. The black waters of the strait seem to sit in ominous silence. Though the lens of my spyglass, I saw

Lady's Revenge *slip over the horizon
at last.*

The next part of the entry had faded badly, and the ink had run. That part of the page was hopelessly indecipherable. Zak could make out the handwriting a bit further down.

> *—doused the deck in what I suspect was kerosene, he set the mess alight. By the time the crew noticed, 'twas far too late.*
> *Eleanor lowered the sole remaining dinghy and had just loosened its ropes and almost managed to heave herself inside when he attacked her.*
> *My hand shakes much.*

The entry ended there and it appeared as if someone had ripped out the next few pages. He'd noticed that had been done earlier in the journal, too.

Zak heaved a frustrated sigh. Seeing that dinghy didn't fit the pattern of the other sightings. Which, in a way, made this journal entry even more legitimate. He closed his eyes and brought to mind the apparition he'd seen.

His brow furrowed. He seemed to recall two figures in the dinghy but then again, he could've just made that up now.

The ping of an incoming text message on his phone made him open his eyes. He glanced down. Granddad. *Zak. Emergency family meeting. I need you to come up to Dalvay as soon as you can.* His granddad, Ian Stuart, always did have a flair for the dramatic. When he said emergency family meeting, it usually meant he couldn't find his reading glasses.

Ever since Granddad had retired from active treasure hunting, Zak had gotten these messages more frequently. Probably just needed a sense of excitement in his life. *Sure, Granddad. You OK?*

Zak got up off the couch. He was the only family Granddad had now. He'd better head up to the Dalvay estate on the north shore right away. *Right as rain, son. No need to race up here. I'm not dying.*

Zak exhaled in relief. *I need to meet with my team tomorrow so if you're OK with it, I could come up Sunday afternoon?* After a second, his phone dinged. *Sunday's fine. See you then.*

Zak rubbed his eyes. Long days of

searching and diving was making his brain foggy. But he thought he remembered one of his team members had said something about some New Yorker coming aboard for research Sunday morning.

Chapter Three

O N Sunday morning, Maggie drove her rental car along the winding highway that hugged P.E.I.'s south shore. Morning light gleamed off the water and filtered through the pines.

Crap. What had she gotten herself into?

She straightened her shoulders. She wasn't going to feel intimidated to see Zak again. He'd approved it, which meant he was totally fine with this. She was worried for nothing.

Besides, she wasn't going to let her one chance at more success than she'd dreamed of slip away from her just because the person she needed help from happened to be her ex almost-fiancé. Who had ignored her artistic dreams in favor of his own career.

Her hands tightened on the wheel.

She'd stick this out. See it to the end.

Her jewelry design, and her career goals, were worth it. Yes. She'd stay professional. Calm.

Everything would be fine.

She stepped out of her rental car and onto the tiny pier as the wind buffeted her blue striped cotton sundress. A smile formed on her lips.

Even though she hadn't been back here since she'd helped her parents move off-island for retirement, nothing had changed. The scent of pine still lingered in the air. And the cry of gulls still sounded overhead. As the water sparkled in the sunlight, Maggie's heart lifted. Her fingers closed briefly around the antique bracelet, which she'd put in a zippered interior pocket of her purse. Maybe, since she was here anyway, she could try to ask Zak about that verse or stanza or whatever it was…?

Way down at the end of the pier, a dinghy bobbed on the water's surface. And a man in a pale yellow button-down shirt began to walk up the pier. His wavy brown hair ruffled in the breeze.

Maggie adjusted her over-large tortoiseshell sunglasses and wished the glasses hid more of her face. She pulled the wide brim of her straw hat lower. She could do this. Her toes curled in her white Keds as he got closer. Even as she watched him approach, she held her breath.

Oh no. No. No. She couldn't do this.

But before she could turn and run-walk away, Zak stood in front of her. She hadn't seen him since the night she'd refused his proposal and broken his heart for the second time.

The wind gusted and she put one hand on her hat. She swallowed. Her mouth went dry and her palms suddenly felt sweaty. Crap.

"Thanks for agreeing to help me," she finally managed, "with my research for this next piece in my jewelry line," she finished in a rush.

"Maggie." His eyes narrowed. "It was *you* my grad assistant meant." He crossed his arms over his chest. His hazel eyes were cold.

She opened her mouth to reply but no words came out. How did he even know who she was in these giant sunglasses and wide-brimmed hat? Not to mention the hideously wrinkled dress she was wearing.

He must have remembered the sound of her voice. She cleared her throat and went to slide her hands into her pockets. Hide at least some part of herself from his gaze.

But her dress didn't have any pockets. So she fisted her hands at her sides, instead.

Her pulse pounded in her throat and she willed him not to notice. His eyes, however, remained firmly engaged on her face.

Her chest tightened. "So—" she forced the word past the sudden lump in her throat "—where are we going?"

He leaned against one of the pilings but a muscle in his jaw ticked.

He uncrossed his arms and stuffed them into the front pockets of his neatly pressed navy blue Dockers.

She felt like she might throw up. Were those the same pair of pants he'd worn on their second date in university? She thought she recognized the torn left belt loop.

He jerked a thumb to indicate the boat behind them. "As you should already know—" he paused, his tone measured and formal "—the project's out here on the

Northumberland Strait."

God, had it been three years, really?

Her lips compressed in a line.

Three years since he'd ignored her artistic dreams in favor of what was probably yet another dead-end in his tireless hunt for shipwrecks.

A slice of anger surged through her, and she clung to it as if it were a life preserver. She straightened her spine. "Right." Her heart pounded. She held her hands up, palms out. "Believe me, if I'd known I'd receive this kind of...welcome... from you—" she tapped her foot "—I would've never come up here."

Zak shifted his weight. Studied her for one long minute. Then two.

Maggie put her hands on her hips.

Just then, an older man came up behind Zak. Probably his assistant. "Everything's ready to go, Dr. Stuart. This the person we were waiting for?"

Zak gave a curt nod and turned away from Maggie without saying anything else.

Maggie lifted her chin and followed behind the two men.

AFTER THEY BOARDED the research vessel, Zak glanced at her as they crossed the deck. It dipped slightly under Maggie's feet but she kept her balance as she dug out a pen and notepad from her purse.

She had to at least make an attempt to ask him some of the research questions she'd come here for. She straightened her shoulders. Best to start with a broad open-ended one. "So what do you know about female pirates?"

"I'm a scientist, not a historian."

He walked on without waiting for her.

Maggie forced herself to take a slow breath and speak in a calm tone. "The thing is, this ship you're looking for is in the same era as a female pirate I'm interested in learning more about."

"Try Wikipedia."

She fought down a wave of frustration and followed him across the deck. "But my assistant said that you knew something about a female pirate named Eleanor Webster."

"Listen, you're wasting your time. That's not my field."

Her lips compressed. "But surely you have some story about her—" She stopped talking. She'd been naive to think she'd be able to ask him about much of anything, let alone that verse. She shook her head and shoved her pen and notepad back into her purse.

"You think some big, romantic story can stand in for serious research?" He lifted his brows.

Maggie lifted her chin and glared at him.

Zak glared back.

Overhead, a seagull wheeled and called.

Zak blinked. He rubbed the back of his neck then turned to the rail and studied the water for a long moment. "Since you're here," he said at last, "you might as well come take a look at the monitors so you know what it is we're looking for."

"Thank you." She followed him, her back straight, into a small low-ceilinged room where monitors and switches and lights flashed and beeped.

Despite herself, Maggie noticed Zak's scuffed Top-Siders with frayed white laces. A traitorous smile tugged at her lips. He always had loved beat-up old shoes. More comfortable, he said.

When Zak tapped the screen directly

in front of him, she dragged her eyes from his shoes and lifted her chin. "So, what are we looking at, here?"

"Frankly, just sandy sea bottom," Zak said. In the blue glow of the monitor, Maggie saw the worry lines around his eyes. She tamped down a surge of annoyance at herself. His worries were none of her business.

"We're moving the boat a few inches at a time," he explained, "and using robotics and computers to map out the bottom. But until we get the big, clear picture of what we're looking at, we don't know exactly where to search."

Maggie's heart squeezed. He sounded so...formal. Distant. No. Of course he would. He had nothing to do with her personal life any more.

"That was the mistake I made before," Zak muttered under his breath, so softly at first that she didn't think she'd heard right.

But she knew better than to ask him about mistakes. Her gaze traveled to the stacks of files and charts and papers next to the monitors.

"So," Maggie said, "what's the name of the ship? Is there anything I can do here to,

uh, help?" Why was she offering her help? Zak didn't need it. Or want it.

"*Lady's Revenge.*" Zak slid a glance in her direction that she couldn't quite read. "I thought you were the one who needed an expert's help."

An awkward silence ensued.

One of the research assistants poked her head in the doorway. "Zak? We need your input on where to drop the sea floor scanner next."

"Okay." Zak headed out the door.

Fine. If he was going to be uncooperative, the least she could do was get some work done on the drawing. Maggie returned to the deck and the bright wind-tossed sunshine.

But as she did, chatter from some of Zak's team members drifted to her. "Did you hear them arguing?"

A pause. Then, "Seems like there's *something* between them, eh?" the other person said. Maggie paused mid-stride.

"Yeah. I wonder how long they've known each other?"

Maggie's heart lurched as she recalled standing at the railing of Zak's sailboat, his warm embrace warding off the damp sea air.

"They looked kinda cute together, didn't they?" the first person added.

And the way that her heart had leapt to her throat as they'd talked about the future. *Their* future. Sadness rippled through her.

"Maybe there's more going on there...?" The second said.

Maggie took a deep breath. Nothing was going on here. He didn't *get* her. Had never gotten her. Hadn't been supportive of her art, her dreams...

She clenched her jaw and made her way back to the table she'd spotted in the corner of the deck by a pile of ropes and the life jacket storage unit.

She got out her sketchpad and pencil and took a seat.

After twenty minutes with no progress, she looked down at the blank page and sighed. She was not going to acknowledge the way that his memory lingered in her mind the same way that his cologne now lingered on the breeze.

Besides all that, thinking about him wasn't getting anything useful down on paper.

She started at the sketchpad. She'd

drawn some sort of half-circle that was supposed to be a pendant but looked more like something a four-year-old had done at daycare.

She ran a hand through her windblown hair. Tapped her pencil against the sketchpad and looked out at the horizon.

The water lapped at the boat and made her wonder if there was actually any point. What did she want to convey? Feminine power. Passion. Strength. And beauty.

She chewed on the end of the pencil and frowned. Why was this so hard? Maybe she couldn't create something entirely of her own imagination.

Maybe she couldn't be successful unless she had some pattern to follow, some guaranteed sure thing. Her mind strayed back to her charm bracelet tucked into her purse alongside the antique bracelet.

She worried her bottom lip. Maybe she couldn't be successful completely on her own. She had to have someone hold her hand, point her in the direction she should go, rather than follow her own heart.

Her pulse pounded in her ears and she tried to push the negative voices, the negative thoughts, down. But they only grew louder and louder until they were all she could hear.

She threw down her pencil and jumped up from the plastic deck chair. It nearly toppled over as she went to the railing with the sketchpad still clutched in her hand.

She felt the tiniest dip in her stomach as she recalled Zak's avoidance of her—and her questions. But then again, she was the one who'd done it to him. Made him afraid to get close. Afraid to actually *trust* her.

She sighed. She didn't know why she'd bothered. Besides, she had more important things to think about.

She sat down again and picked up her pencil.

Suddenly her phone buzzed. She looked at it. Zak's granddad? She grinned. She'd always liked him. They'd occasionally kept in touch. She answered the call.

ZAK KEPT HIS shoulders straight as he crossed the deck. They'd been out here the whole morning and found nothing. Some archaeologist he was.

His lips twisted into a wry smile. Now Maggie could see how close they were to not finding anything... He forced his thoughts away from that. From her.

He clenched his teeth. Maggie. He hadn't seen her since she'd refused his proposal. His hands fisted at his sides. The ding of an incoming text made him glance at his phone. *So how many gold bars can I tell the publisher you picked up on your dive? (Kidding, kidding! But I hope you have good news for me about the boat.)*

He rubbed the back of his neck. How was he going to tell his agent that he hadn't made any progress on finding the ship? That the last chapter still hadn't been written?

He glanced at his Hublot. Just about time to head to Dalvay to meet with Granddad. He texted his research assistant to make sure the dinghy would be brought back to the boat.

"Listen," he said as he found Maggie near the back of the boat, "I have somewhere to be. But feel free to spend the rest of the day out here if you like. Take notes, whatnot." He made an expansive gesture.

Maggie put her hands on her hips.

"Notes on what? I'm researching Eleanor Webster, not nautical archaeology."

Zak shifted his weight. "I don't know much about her."

Maggie narrowed her eyes at him. "You could at least tell me what you *do* know instead of avoiding me."

"I'm not avoiding you. I'm trying to find a damn shipwreck. Why do you want to know about this female pirate anyway?"

"She's going to be the inspiration for a new piece of jewelry I'm, uh," Maggie bit her lip, "supposed to be designing."

Zak glanced at his watch.

"Well, fine then," Maggie tapped her foot. "Go on and do...whatever you need to. I'll see if one of your colleagues is more forthcoming." She wheeled around and walked away.

Zak bit back a retort and headed to the dinghy. His research assistant helped him undo its moorings. He wasn't avoiding—He sighed. Okay. He *was* avoiding her. But how could he bring himself to admit he knew so little about Eleanor?

He shook his head and piloted the dinghy back to the pier. After he handed off the boat to his assistant to take back to the

research vessel, he headed to his pickup and up the highway to Dalvay.

At the Dalvay estate, he made his way across the lush expanse of lawn. The big sandstone-and-timber Victorian home that sat on the property faced the Gulf of St. Lawrence.

Alexander MacDonald had built the huge house in 1897 on 120 acres and had named it Dalvay-by-the-Sea.

Zak chuckled. MacDonald had intended the place as a summer cottage. A plaque now designated MacDonald's home as a Canadian National Historic Site.

Dormer windows with graceful white-painted eaves dominated the roofline and English Tudor-style beams framed the gable ends. Clusters of tourists sat in the Adirondack chairs and wicker settees on the wide white-pillared verandah. Zak went around the back of the wide wrap-around porch.

A little way off, smaller cottages dotted the property. They'd been added in the 1950s when the MacDonald family couldn't afford to keep the estate and it had been converted into a resort.

Granddad liked to rent one of the small

cottages during the summertime. He'd been doing that for years and this summer was no different.

"Hi Granddad."

"Zak, you made it!"

Sunshine streamed past the heavy wood girding. The older man, with once-jet-black hair now nearly silver, sat on a wicker chair with yellow chintz cushions. He wore cheap plastic reading glasses and a silk bowtie emblazoned with navy blue anchors.

"Good to see you." Zak hugged him then raised his eyebrows. "But what's with all the theatrics? And the bowtie?"

"A tribute to the occasion, son."

"You didn't lose your reading glasses again, did you?"

Zak's grandfather chuckled and adjusted his glasses. "Went to Shopper's Drug Mart and got myself a new pair this time." He glanced around and lowered his voice. "But seriously, Zak, you might want to sit down for this."

Zak threw his grandfather a rather speculative look and sat down in a matching wicker chair across from him. Zak opened his mouth, but Granddad

raised a hand before he could speak. "Please. Just listen this time, okay? And if you could set aside your, shall we say... healthy skepticism, I'd appreciate it."

MAGGIE BREATHED A sigh of relief as she drove her rented sedan down the highway. It'd been a good idea to get off the boat— she'd left not long after Zak.

Zak's colleagues hadn't known too many details about Eleanor. They'd told her Eleanor had been mentioned in some travel journal Zak had. Aside from that, they'd all said to talk to Zak.

Zak's grandfather, on the other hand, had asked her to come up to see him this afternoon; after he'd heard what she was working on, he'd said he had something to tell her about Eleanor. What kind of information *would* he have about her? She felt a tingle of excitement.

She glanced at her folder full of sup-posedly-inspiring pictures—some ripped from magazines, some taken with her own Nikon—on the seat beside her and smiled.

It felt good to be back on the island.

Something about the salt air revived her. No, restored her...soul.

ZAK SHIFTED IN the wicker chair.

His grandfather leaned forward. "I didn't think what I'm about to say was relevant to your work. But, well, I recently learned that ship you're looking for is called *Lady's Revenge*. Not only that, after talking with a certain young woman we both know, I've come to realize a few things and I hope that means you've come around."

"Granddad," Zak frowned, "you're not going to tell me that story again about—"

"My father and the original owner of this place? Yes, I am. Because you see, there are a few details I never shared."

"If you think I'm suddenly going to believe you and go off on some wild treasure hunt, then you can think again." Zak crossed his arms. "That's why I went into nautical archaeology. Science and facts, not here-say and pipe dreams."

"Oh, so nautical archaeologists don't have theories or speculations?" A twinkle gleamed in Ian's eyes. "Wreck diving seems an awful lot like treasure hunting to me. You *were* the assistant to the nautical archaeologist who found Captain Kidd's ship *Adventure Galley* three years ago."

"I was a PhD student back then." Zak's jaw tightened. "And that was based on years of research, time and effort."

"And treasure hunting isn't? Besides, aren't you, right now, looking for the shipwreck that's supposed to be the Ghost Ship of the Northumberland Strait?"

Zak gave a huff of irritation. "Treasure hunters aren't the same as archaeologists. If the treasure hunters aren't trained, they risk damaging the historical and cultural significance of a site, of an artifact. They're looking for gold, valuables. They want money, fame... Glory." A muscle in his jaw twitched. "I care about the history, the science, the stories of the people behind the objects and the sites. Treasure hunters—" Zak shook his head "—their emphasis is completely skewed." He crossed his arms and frowned.

Zak's grandfather set his jaw. "Listen, Zak, I didn't ask you here to debate viewpoints and perspectives. I asked you here to listen to me." He cleared his throat and his tone became somewhat stern. "Can you please do me the favor of that much?"

Zak tugged on his earlobe. "Yes, Granddad." He scuffed the toe of one shoe against the wide oak floorboards.

"Thank you." The older man reached into the breast pocket of his faded gingham shirt and pulled out a small white envelope folded and refolded so many times that its edges had creased and frayed.

He put it on the small table between the two chairs but kept his fingers on its edge.

"When my father, your great-grandfather, James P. Stuart, was a young man in his twenties, he worked for the man who built this place—Alexander MacDonald, once president of Standard Oil alongside John D. Rockefeller. Your great-grandfather became MacDonald's most trusted employee. Over the ten years Dad worked here at Dalvay, MacDonald saw how much he loved the area, and they developed a great friendship—"

Zak drummed his fingers on the chair's arm. He'd heard this before too many times to count. "That's when you mention the part where Samuel Stuart wrote the Beale Papers, which supposedly." Zak made air quotes, "leads to some sort of vast treas—"

The older man shot Zak a piercing look. "Son, just hold on a minute longer will you?"

Zak inhaled then exhaled slowly. Nodded.

"One summer evening," Ian continued, "when Rockefeller came up to Dalvay to visit MacDonald, Dad overheard MacDonald tell Rockefeller about a letter in his possession written by the famous pirate Captain Kidd."

Zak stopped drumming his fingers.

"Unfortunately, the letter was only a fragment."

Zak leaned forward.

Ian went on. "Nicholas MacDonald, Alexander's great-grandfather, received that letter from Kidd when Kidd was in jail."

Zak's brows rose. "He did?"

"Before Kidd was executed in 1701 for piracy," Ian added.

"Really?"

"It turns out—" the older man cleared

his throat again "—that Nicholas served aboard two ships. One, Captain Kidd's ship *Adventure Galley*. The other ship—" Zak's grandfather held Zak's gaze "—*Lady's Revenge.*"

Despite himself, Zak drew in a sharp breath.

"So Alexander inherited that letter," the older man continued, "or what was left of it. But it ended up in my father's possession after Dad told Alexander of his own connection to the Beale Papers, through my grandfather, your great-great-grandfather, Samuel Stuart."

The older man tapped his fingers against the worn envelope. Picked it up. Carefully opened it. A small Ziploc bag lay in his palm. Two fragments were encased in the protective plastic.

The pieces were old. Zak cocked his head. *Really* old.

On the first fragment, which looked deliberately torn, was a faded, yet still discernible, signature.

Wm Kidd

Zak's eyes widened then darted to the other piece of the antique letter. The second segment was larger. Zak silently read the faded penmanship:

Newgate Prison   London, England
20 May 1701   Nicholas MacDonald

My loyal Friend,

Your Aide is the last and only to which I now appeal. Neither Bellomont nor Harley believed nor heeded my requests for clemency and so I turn to you. 'Tis too late, I fear, for my own life to be spared, but I pray I may count on you to honor one last Request of mine.

I feel I owe Eleanor. As you are already in Eleanor's employ on Lady's Revenge, I trust that you make way in the North Atlantic. Mayhap even toward that fair land the French call St. John's Island.

If that is indeed the Case, though she is no longer under my command, I swore I would give Eleanor no more do—

Zak's eyes traced the torn edge. Another mention of *Lady's Revenge*? By Kidd himself? His pulse sped up but his frown deepened.

"Seems to me," Ian said, "this letter indicates Nicholas's deathbed confession about 'an island east of Boston' meant P.E.I."

"So this letter is why Dad thought he'd be able to find more of Kidd's treasure on P.E.I.," Zak said.

Ian sighed and nodded. "But the question is, Zak, what do *you* think about the letter?

Zak threw his granddad a look. "It seems like a lot of conjecture to me. I mean, Kidd doesn't directly *say* there's some sort of treasure. Kidd doesn't even know for sure that Nicholas was headed for St. John's Island—what's now P.E.I. But what would Eleanor have to do with all of that anyway?"

And yet...

Could this lead somewhere? Zak's heart began to race. But he clenched his jaw and shifted in his seat. Zak cocked his head. "Why are you telling me all this?"

"Because I want you to have it." Ian held out the plastic bag but Zak didn't take it. "I want to pass this piece of my legacy on to you before I kick the bucket. And I thought you'd appreciate it—heck, it might even help you—what with this very serious ghost ship research you're doing." He chuckled then punched some buttons on his cell phone.

He held out the bag again to Zak. "It's our legacy."

"It's not a legacy, Granddad. It's a hoax." He scuffed the toe of his shoe against the floorboards again. "Besides, this letter wasn't mentioned in anything published about the Beale Papers."

"Of course it wasn't." Ian wiggled his eyebrows. "They didn't know about it. You know what else they didn't know? That Samuel wrote the Beale Papers—anonymously—so that people wouldn't bust down his door looking for treasure."

Zak stood abruptly. "People—like our relatives—have searched unsuccessfully for years for Kidd's supposed treasure and have sunk millions of dollars into it." He shoved his hands into his pockets. "I'm sorry, Granddad. I love you but I have, as you say, this very serious shipwreck I'm looking for and a book to finish writing. I'm not getting involved in this."

"Well," the older man replied, "fifteen years, I'm sorry to see, hasn't changed your mind any. In fact," he rubbed his forehead, "it's only made things worse." He got up out of his chair too and walked over to the edge of the porch. "But I thought—" he beckoned to someone across the lawn "—at the very least, since Maggie told me she's doing research on Eleanor Webster, the two of you might want to look at the letter together."

MAGGIE LIFTED HER fingers in a half-wave at Ian and smiled—a genuine one. "Mr. Stuart! It's great to see you. I'm so glad you said you could help me out." She avoided looking at Zak and shifted her folder to her other arm.

"So, what do you have there?" Ian asked. "All your information about Eleanor?"

She laughed. "Oh! No, this is for my jewelry ideas and inspirations." She held up the folder.

"Good for you." The older man sat down again at the same time that Maggie

walked up onto the porch.

Zak leaned stiffly against the porch railing as Maggie settled into the chair opposite Ian. She ignored Zak.

Ian glanced between Maggie and Zak. "You sure finding out more about Eleanor's the only reason for your visit to the island?" Ian gave Maggie a wink.

"Oh, well, I'm—" Maggie looked down and tugged at her skirt.

"She's spending some time on my boat doing research for some jewelry project she's working on." The deep, rich timbre of Zak's voice cut into Maggie's heart.

Maggie crossed her arms.

Zak shifted his weight and stared out across the lawn.

Maggie pulled out a pen and notepad from her purse. "So, what's this about Eleanor, Mr. Stuart?"

"Well, Maggie..." He drew in a deep breath. "I was trying to give Zak a family heirloom of sorts, but he isn't having it."

Maggie peered down at the plastic bag in Zak's granddad's weathered hands.

"Don't go getting her involved in this," Zak said and crossed his arms too. "She'll just use it against us later."

"I'm not getting her involved," the older man said. "I'm only asking her if she wants to join us." He held up the plastic baggie and offered it to her.

"I told you *I* don't want to get involved." Zak said. "She shouldn't, either. Complete waste of time."

"What is?" Maggie repeated as she took the Ziploc bag.

"No, don't—" Zak began.

"—A fragment of a letter from Captain Kidd." The older man threw an impatient look at his grandson. "Involving some lost treasure on P.E.I. that our family's been searching for, and a woman named Eleanor."

"Really?" Maggie's eyes widened as she read the fragment. What did Kidd owe Eleanor? And how had she ended up on or near P.E.I.?

"Wow!" She looked up at Ian after she'd finished reading. "This is...an amazing piece of information." She jotted down some notes. "Thank you, Mr. Stuart, for showing me."

She darted a glance at Zak and fiddled with the folder in her lap. One of the glossy pictures slipped out and onto the floor.

As Maggie leaned down to pick up the fallen photo, Ian eyed the picture—an emerald-studded cuff. "Emeralds..." Ian looked intrigued. "Like the Pendant of the Pure Hearted. Another missing Island treasure." He chuckled. "Never know, it might even be part of Kidd's haul."

Zak tsked. "That's just another ridiculous Island legend. There is no pendant, just like there's no treasure."

"And no ghost ship?" Ian raised his eyebrows at Zak and continued. "The pendant's said to be a large emerald. It's also supposed to tell the wearer whether the love they have for someone is true and lasting. Pure hearted, shall we say."

"Well," Mr. Stuart added, "I've never read the story myself but I've heard there is an article about this particular gem somewhere in an early issue of *The Prince Edward Island Magazine*..."

"There is?" Maggie said. But the two men weren't listening to her.

"You know that's all made up, Granddad. They wrote those things in that magazine for entertainment. And—"

"How do you know unless you've read it, Zak?" Mr. Stuart retorted.

"Listen, Mr. Stuart," Maggie broke in. "I'd love to help. But this seems like it's between you and Zak." She bit her lip and stood up. "I'm sorry. I have a big deadline this week and I need to focus on that."

She pivoted on her heel and walked back the way she'd come.

As she slid behind the wheel of her rental car, guilt knotted in her stomach. She'd already done too much when she'd used the Stuart family story for her bracelet. She couldn't get involved with some treasure hunt. Especially not with Zak.

Maggie sighed. Zak wasn't being any help with her research about Eleanor. And while this letter fragment had shown her Eleanor was mentioned elsewhere, it wasn't exactly conclusive. It didn't give much in the way of additional information she needed about the pirate, either. So why was she even here on the island now? Maybe she should just go back to New York.

She put the key in the ignition and started the car.

No. She couldn't leave. She wouldn't give up that easily. There had to be more information out there somewhere about Eleanor. This letter fragment proved that, at least. But maybe she should put Eleanor aside, for awhile anyway, and look into other options? It wouldn't hurt anything.

Like that emerald? She didn't want to hop from one thing to the next but the gem sounded like it had a story behind it that might work really well for the second piece in the line. Hmmm. Maybe if she looked into that, it might turn up something? She tapped a finger against her chin.

Yes.

She put the car into drive. It would be a place to start.

Chapter Four

ZAK SIGHED AND rubbed his neck. He opened one of the windows in the living room then rested his head against the cool leather of the couch and squeezed his eyes shut.

He blew out a breath. Seeing Maggie today on the boat and then at Dalvay had been harder than he'd expected.

His cell phone dinged with a new text message. His gut churned but he ignored the phone. Zak hadn't replied to his agent's earlier text. So it was probably another prod from the guy about Zak's progress on the last chapter of this damn book.

His hands tightened into fists even as his mind wandered back to earlier in the day. The way that Maggie's dark brown hair blew across her forehead. The way his fingers had itched, for one tiny moment, to tuck her hair behind her ear. And the way

she'd broken his heart.

He shook his head. He might as well do something useful like get things down on paper for this last chapter instead of wallowing in memories. Question was, what?

A light breeze blew in through the window as he put on his pair of white cotton gloves. He picked up Davies' journal and opened it at random. He frowned and set it down again, still open. His lips pursed. At the very least, he could do an outline of the research he'd done.

He returned his attention to the blinking cursor on his blank document screen. This final chapter wasn't going to write itself.

The breeze rustled the journal pages.

He fisted his hands into his hair. But where the hell was he going to begin?

He glanced at Davies' journal again. A sudden wind gust caused a single page to turn over and reveal an earlier entry.

3 Jan 1698

Reached the Malabar Coast nigh three days ago.

I must confess, I have not seen

more compelling a creature than Miss Eleanor Webster, now that I've come aboard Adventure Galley.

Though she avoids all my forays into discerning her home and origins, I cannot help but ruminate on such matters, as the rather hunted look in her eyes bespoke volumes to me during our chance encounter last eventide on the quarter-deck.

Though she did not hold her consul this day when she spoke to our captain, one William Kidd, of her need for procuring a new ship of her own—

But the entry ended there, thanks to seawater damage, and Zak could see, it had been hastily blotted, as if the writer had been interrupted in his task.

He stared at the last line: *...a new ship...* His mind raced back to the letter fragment: *As you are already under Eleanor's employ...*

"Of course," Zak muttered under his breath.

He should've paid attention to this entry in connection with his search for the ghost ship when he'd read the journal

initially. He didn't like to miss details. He shifted his weight. But maybe he'd become so focused on *Lady's Revenge*, that he hadn't seen the value of Eleanor's personal story... Because this entry spelled out that Eleanor wanted her *own* ship. That ship must have been *Lady's Revenge*. Which meant that Eleanor wasn't just a crew member on *Lady's Revenge*. She was the captain. Kidd's letter fragment cross-referenced this perfectly.

He turned the page over. Hmm. This was that one that seemed oddly thick. He rubbed the paper between thumb and forefinger and lifted up the journal. But before he could investigate further, his cell phone rang. He grabbed it up without glancing at the caller ID.

"Zak here."

For a second, there was no response. But then he heard the sound of a throat being cleared and a very familiar voice.

His heart sped up and his jaw clenched.

"Zak, please don't hang up on me. I know we've had some...opposing views in the past but—"

"How did you get my number, Maggie?" He fought to keep his voice calm.

"Your granddad was—"

"—Always too forgiving." Zak swore under his breath.

"Zak," Maggie said. Her voice sounded strained. Zak felt a twinge of guilt. Why was he acting like this? He took a centering breath. Forced his tone to be formal. Professionally distant. "I'm sorry. That was unfair. What can I help you with?"

"Well, I debated whether to call you, seeing as how we're, uh... But it kept niggling at me. I can't leave without at least trying to look into this as much as I can. Your colleagues said, in your research on the ship, you'd come across some travel journals with Eleanor Webster mentioned in them. They weren't able to tell me much. So. What do *you* know about her? And don't think about avoiding me this time."

Zak rubbed a hand across his jaw. He wasn't being fair to her. He winced. What would it hurt to share what he'd found about Eleanor? Eleanor wasn't his focus, after all; the ship was.

"In around 1701, she was apparently the love interest of a fur trader and explorer named Henry Davies. Before I

found his journal at an estate sale up in Georgetown, the crew manifests of *Adventure Galley* were key to my making the connection between Eleanor and Kidd."

"Okay," Maggie said. "But I thought you didn't care about Eleanor."

Zak shoved his free hand in his pocket and bit back a retort. Instead, he said. "Davies mentions in his journal that Eleanor talked to Kidd about a new ship for herself. That new ship? Was *Lady's Revenge.*"

"Wow. What else?"

"Well," Zak added, unable to help the excited note that crept into his voice, "My original theory was that Eleanor, after she parted ways with Kidd, became a crew member on *Lady's Revenge*. I didn't think too much about her. But it turns out she was the captain." He didn't have to tell Maggie he'd *just* made that discovery.

"I could've told you that."

"Wait, what?"

"You never asked me what *I* knew about Eleanor."

Zak shifted his weight.

Maggie cleared her throat.

"No," Zak admitted at last, "I didn't." After a moment, he added, almost to himself, "I pretty much made educated guesses about things that could've used a little more education. Maybe if I hadn't done that, I wouldn't be up a creek now." He lowered his voice. Ashamed to admit it?

"That's tough," she said.

"Especially when you haven't finished the last chapter for a book that could be worth a five figure advance..."

"Oh?"

Zak shrugged. "I'm sure I'll get it done. I just need to find the damn wreck by the start of next month."

"Well, if you need any, uh, help..." She trailed off and then rushed on before he could say anything else. "By the way, you know anything more about the Pendant of the Pure Hearted?"

Zak crossed his arms. "I'm a serious nautical archaeologist. I don't do research on local legends."

Maggie snorted. "Right. How else would you find out about the ghost ship?"

A strained chuckle escaped Zak. "Always perceptive, Maggie." A long time ago,

he'd liked that about her. The way she cut to the heart of the matter. Zak winced. Focus. Deep breaths. He could do this.

"I'm sorry." There. That was civil. Pleasant, even. "I don't know anything else about it. And I'd take Granddad's treasure story—along with his mention of that article in *The Prince Edward Island Magazine*—with a grain of salt."

MONDAY AT NOON, Maggie took the last bite of her deviled ham sandwich, brushed the crumbs off her denim capris then tossed the empty bag into the trashcan by the biography section in Charlottetown's Confederation Centre public library.

She rolled her shoulders. As she waited for the librarian to return, her mind wandered back to yesterday. The look in Zak's eyes as his granddad had talked about the treasure and the letter fragment. *Pendant of the Pure Hearted.* The words kept rolling through her mind. But she hadn't gotten hold of Mr. Stuart to ask him anything more about it.

Which is why she'd ended up here.

Maggie chewed her lip. She hadn't wanted to impose. He wasn't almost-family any more. She had no business asking him for anything. Even though when he'd called her on the boat, he'd insisted she take Zak's cell phone number, too... She twirled a lock of hair around her finger. For strictly professional purposes, of course. But Zak hadn't been much help about the pendant, either. She glanced at the clock. Ten minutes had gone by.

The elevator dinged at last.

A tall, thin man in his late sixties, with wire-rimmed glasses and a green-checked shirt, reappeared. He held a cloth-bound volume with frayed corners. A red sticker read *non-circulating* on the book's spine.

"So that pendant story appears in *The Prince Edward Island Magazine, Volume I.* These volumes—" he tapped the cover "—are great resources because they are collections of every article published from that magazine in the early days of Island life."

He paused. "What's more, no one really references these books. You can't check them out, either. Hardly anyone—including some of the younger staff members—knows the library has these volumes because they're so rarely requested. I'm pretty much the only one left on staff who knows." The reference librarian flipped through the age-spotted pages until he reached page 277. "Now, this pendant tale is one few Islanders know about but—"

Maggie's cell phone dinged. She ignored it.

"—it's one they should *all* know about. Because, well..." He handed her the book. "I'll let you read it yourself."

As Maggie took the book, a faint mustiness wafted to her. She glanced down at the reprinted article.

April 1848 A Missing Pendant Vol. I, No. 1

It was well nigh some seventy-odd years ago that this happened. I myself was just a young lad no taller than my grand-pap's knee. But oh, I have a keen memory and a sharp mind. I still remember, clear as day, that cold winter night.

Grand-pap told the tale of himself being a young man no more than 21, and a sailor in the days when tall ships still ruled the seas.

"I solemnly swear this is the full and honest truth, now, lad," my grand-pap said to me. He looked at me with his clear blue eyes and the crackle of the flames in the hearth seemed to jump along with his words:

"See, I was a captain in the Royal Navy and had many strange happenings occur. When I served on a ship called The Patagonia *in the year 1701, a huge storm blew up one evening out of a clear, star-filled sky. Off in the distance, as the rain lashed down, I could see an orange-ish glow. A shade of orange that strikes fear into the heart of every sailor. A fire ship. And 'twas heading straight for us.*

So I get the idea to set up a sort of bucket brigade. As the flaming ship drew nearer—it came almost stem to stern with The Patagonia*—I jumped aboard the flaming ship, buckets in hand, and began to douse the flames.*

That's when I saw, through the billowing smoke, a tall silhouette. The figure wore a tricorn hat and a captain's jacket with brass buttons that

gleamed in the moonlight despite the cloud cover. I nearly dropped the buckets.

I fumbled for the hilt of my sword. But the woman in the tricorn hat merely laughed. I could see, as the clouds parted for a moment, her sea-green eyes flash emerald in the starlight. She was the most beautiful woman I'd ever seen.

The flames danced and twisted around her. Her raven-dark hair was coiled into a tight braid that formed a crown around her head. And a jagged scar ran down her left cheek.

Though my lungs began to fill with the burning, acrid smoke, I managed to choke out, "Who are you?" The woman touched a necklace at her throat. Diamond and emerald rings flashed on her fingers as she did.

Finally, she spoke, in a whisper-soft voice that commanded my attention with its sweet chiming sound. "Though my eye color and manner in which I dress my hair give cause for others to call me an emerald queen, my name is Eleanor Webster. Do not try to save us, foolish man. We are in far graver danger than some leather buckets filled with seawater could ever douse."

I began to cough at that point, as the flames crackled even higher. "But," Eleanor said—her voice reached my ears despite the wind, waves and flames—"your heart is pure. For that, you shall be rewarded. Though you are not the first man who has been taken by my beauty."

I did not know what to answer. My eyes came to rest on the necklace around her throat. "Ah," she said, "You admire the piece? I met a wise woman—once a maharani—who gifted me the central pendant. She told of its power to discern true love. She saw within me what others did not, could not; that I had a pure heart. Here," she said, and raised her hands to the sparkling necklace at her throat. Her expression saddened as her fingers brushed the heart-shaped gap in the necklace.

"Take the remaining gem—I need

it not. Though 'tis not the central pendant, may it still serve you as reminder: do not allow your course of true love to be thwarted, as I did. Perhaps you, then, shall not be forced to pay for your mistakes in such a manner thus."

She waved one hand at the flames while the other twisted the final gem from the necklace and handed it to me. "Do not forget," she called as the smoke closed in around her. Well, I wasted no time.

I leapt across the rail to my own ship and caught onto the yardarm just as billows of smoke obscured the strange, doomed vessel. And in the last moments before my feet touched The Patagonia's decking, I thought I heard her voice on the wind. "For I became more concerned about the trappings of love than with being with my dearest."

When I looked again, as I blinked against the sting of smoke and sea spray, I saw that the flaming ship had completely...disappeared. Yet some- how I still clutched the gem in my hand.

"And so, my dear boy," my grand-pap said to me, as he gazed into the dancing flames, "that is the tale of a missing pendant, a phantom ship and a pirate queen."

My mouth hung open, and as I looked up at him I recall that I said, "But Grand-pap, what happened to the queen? And the missing pendant?" But my grand-pap just shook his head. "Lad, if I knew that, I'd be a richer man than most. No one knows what happened to either. Not even I."

Maggie looked up from the aged pages, her eyes wide. So Eleanor was a ghost, just like her ship, *Lady's Revenge*. And at one point, she'd also had the pendant.

Maggie's heart pounded. This was... She scrambled for her notebook and a pen. Exactly the inspiration she needed. Hmmm. Eleanor seemed to like jewelry. She'd had the necklace. Did that mean maybe she'd had something to do with the antique bracelet, or at least, that coin on the bracelet, at one point, too?

But then she frowned. Glanced at the

passage again. Why did part of the passage seem familiar?

She paused. Re-read it.

Right. That *Petticoats & Pistols* book. But that had only been a small section. A sort of modified excerpt, she realized. Surely they would've listed this in the bibliography?

The bibliography. She rubbed her temples.

In all the excitement, she'd completely forgotten to check the back of that book. Well, it didn't matter now. She'd found the original source. She grinned and took photos of the pages with her phone.

Then she gently closed the musty book and handed it back to the reference librarian. "That's quite the story." This would be the perfect jumping-off point for the story behind the second piece. "Can I make a photocopy of this?" She'd add the paper copy to her inspiration folder.

The librarian took the book from her. "I can do that for you here, actually." He ran the copier and then handed the still-warm pages to her. "Are you working on some research then?"

"Oh," Maggie answered. "Yes..." There

had to be more about Eleanor here... "Do you know anything more about this pendant that's mentioned?"

The reference librarian adjusted his glasses. "In the thirty years I've been on staff here, that's the only reference to it that I've ever heard of." He frowned. "But let me make a call."

He punched some numbers on his desk phone. "Hi Beth, it's Jerry at the Confed Centre library. How are ya? Mmm-hmmm. Oh, did she now? That's great. Congratulations!"

Maggie tapped her foot.

"Listen, I have someone here asking about that pendant story in *The Prince Edward Island Magazine, Volume I.*"

A pause. Then, "No, no. I didn't think so." He shook his head. "Right. Thanks anyway."

Jerry hung up the phone and turned to Maggie. "I just called the public archives. Unfortunately, that's the only piece of information we have about the pendant. And they don't know anyone who might know anything else."

"Oh." Maggie tried to ignore the ping of disappointment in her stomach. "Well, thanks anyway."

"Sure. Glad to help," the reference librarian said, before he turned back to his computer.

Maggie pulled out her phone and scanned the message that had come in earlier. It was from Jia at the Courtney Jewelers. *How's the sketch coming? We're looking forward to seeing the preliminaries on Friday.*

Maggie's mouth went dry. Was she relying too much on waiting for inspiration to strike? No. No. This was legitimate research. This would give her what she needed in order to create the drawing.

She couldn't draw just anything. This was Courtney Jewelers. It had to be perfect.

ZAK'S PHONE RANG. He answered it without thinking.

"I just forwarded an article to you," Maggie said.

"Article?"

"That article your granddad mentioned."

"About what?"

"Do you want to help me find it?"

"Find what?"

"The pendant."

Zak fisted a hand in his hair. "Even if I believed it was real—which I don't—" he smiled despite himself "—I'm too busy."

"And," Maggie continued as if she hadn't heard him, "if we found it, I'd be willing to split the proceeds fifty-fifty."

"Right." Zak frowned. "I'm not a treasure hunter. The answer is no."

"But—"

He hung up. Then glanced at the text he hadn't looked at earlier. It was from his agent.

Just got out of a meeting with the publisher. Sorry, but they've changed their minds about buying the manuscript, Zak. No hard feelings? Remember, no contract was signed. It was only in talks, after all. Publishing's cutthroat—they can't wait around forever on an incomplete book. I could try to shop your nearly-complete manuscript around somewhere else but to be honest, I'm not sure it's worth my time. So we'll need to part ways.

Zak resisted the urge to punch something. Instead, he stood up and stalked out to the deck. He gripped the railing. Now what was he going to do about future funding?

He sighed and turned his attention to his phone.

Absently, he opened the photos he'd received from Maggie and read the pages. He knew exactly why he hadn't seen the story about the pendant before. And why he wouldn't have paid attention, if he had.

Because it was just another lost-treasure legend. With no basis in fact...

He exhaled. A pirate queen on a burning ship. He shook his head. A burning ship...that had vanished? And Eleanor? As he finished the passage, his pulse began to race. There was no way—

He re-read the date of the sighting. The year 1701?

He flipped back through his notebooks on the earliest phantom ship sightings. No. This one wasn't listed. Which meant, this was the very first sighting.

How had he missed this account in all the time he'd spent doing research? Probably because it had mainly to do with that supposed pendant.

He looked up from his notebooks. Maybe he could use some of *The Patago-*

nia's logbooks—if any still existed—to pinpoint the location of the wreck?

He glanced down at the coffee table. Eyed the worn leather of Davies' travel journal.

Hmmm.

Davies had seen the real ship that became the legendary phantom, too... So this piece in *The Prince Edward Island Magazine* was more proof that *Lady's Revenge*, which burned in 1701, was the Ghost Ship of the Northumberland Strait.

He drew in a sharp breath. Davies had mentioned Kidd, too. And Kidd had mentioned Eleanor. Not that he was going to believe Granddad's treasure stories, but...

He tapped a finger against his chin.

Could he help Maggie look for this supposed pendant? Would that help him to find the wreck?

But if he did help Maggie, he might, at the very least, gather more evidence about the ship, since the pendant was connected to Eleanor. And Eleanor was connected to *Lady's Revenge*. And in the best case, he could uncover the wreck.

Which would prove completely that

the ghost ship was real. If he did that, he could finish the book. Sell it to some other publisher, even? Gain back that wider exposure and funding he was looking for.

Because if one had been interested, that surely meant another would be, agent or no agent. Hell, he might even publish it himself.

Yes.

Helping out Maggie—and perhaps indirectly, his grandfather—was the answer he was looking for, after all.

TUESDAY MORNING, MAGGIE sat at the back of the boat with her hands in the pockets of her white shorts as she looked to the horizon.

She couldn't help but remember the way the glow of firelight had danced over Zak's bare chest as they'd come out to Bay Fortune on his boat one August night...

A splash and the sound of climbing pulled Maggie's thoughts to the present.

"Find anything?" one of the assistants called as Zak climbed aboard. His dry suit dripped water onto the white deck.

Maggie's breath hitched as Zak's fingers moved to the diagonal zipper pull on the front of the suit.

But she couldn't look away as he tugged the zipper downward.

The slow slide of the zipper brought to mind the taste of chocolate and marshmallow as they'd kissed on that sand bar. Ate so many s'mores by the driftwood fire that their hands were covered in sticky marshmallow...

Zak stepped out of the neoprene dry suit.

Heat rose to Maggie's cheeks.

Oh, those kisses... her eyes fluttered closed. The tenderness beneath each touch. The soft promise of care, of *love*, behind each—

"Maggie, look."

Her eyes flew open. Found Zak's hazel gaze regarded her with curiosity.

She hastily sat more upright. But instantly regretted it. Because now she felt far too close to the strong lines of his chest outlined against the thin white polyester under-suit he had worn beneath the dry suit.

She swallowed. "Uh..." Wet her lips.

Blinked. "Oh, what am I looking at?" Her gaze flicked over his chest, at the way his collarbone dipped in at the base of his throat where his pulse beat. At the way his shirt perfectly set off his slight tan.

Zak held out a tiny misshapen object encrusted in barnacles and silt. As he leaned toward her, she inhaled the scent of fresh laundry and saltwater that clung to him.

"Musket ball from the 17th century," he said. Grinned. And the flash of excitement, joy and...something else... in his eyes, tugged at her.

Reminded her how carefree he'd been when they'd been growing up together. The way the wind buffeted his hair as he stood at the helm of his sailboat, a boyish grin on his face.

The way he'd always given her the first slice of lemon cake he baked even though it was his favorite flavor.

Or the way he'd share an idea with her, then lean back and close his eyes so he could shut out all other distractions in order to take the time to listen—really listen—to her response.

She always could share openly with

him. A lump rose in her throat as she studied the flecks of gold combined with the moss-green in his hazel eyes. Wished she could do something, say something that would bring it all back.

Bring *him* back to her.

Her breath hitched again and she swallowed hard.

This wasn't the past. This was now.

"What, uh, does that mean? How does a single musket ball signify finding *Lady's Revenge*?"

"It doesn't, in and of itself. But it does mean there just might be a debris trail, which could lead us straight to the ship. We find more artifacts like this, we just might be one step closer to finding the wreck." Zak grinned at her. "Join me tonight for a bit of a celebratory meal?"

THE PINKS, PURPLES and golds of sunset glinted on the water just visible from the table at Sheltered Harbour Cafe. Zak fidgeted with the band of his Hublot and finished the last of his fresh-caught clams. Was he actually going to admit to Maggie that he'd decided to help her out?

He rolled up the sleeves of his dark green polished cotton dress shirt then pushed aside his plate and glanced across the table at her. Yes. It would help out both of them. It was the logical thing to do. Her chocolate-brown hair framed her face and set off the lavender scoop-neck lace-edged sundress she wore.

He forced himself to look away, the sight not just filling him with a tug of attraction but also with a morsel of...regret that had somehow pushed aside his anger.

He took a sip of his lemonade. "Tide's out. Evenings like this are perfect for digging clams," he said, almost to himself.

"Remember the time we went to Tea Hill beach and that group of tourists thought we were an actual clam digging company?"

Zak allowed himself a smile. "I think it was because of the logo on my T-shirt."

"Or that brand new shovel I had." Maggie smiled too.

Zak held Maggie's gaze.

"Oh!" Maggie said, "remember that story your half-crazy uncle told us our second year of high school?"

Zak nodded. "About the cache of pearls that went down on the *Molly Mae* in 1769, the year after Charlottetown was founded. We spent that entire summer with a metal detector and a shovel digging on practically every beach along the South Shore."

Maggie laughed. "We really didn't know what we were doing, did we?"

Zak joined in, and shook his head. "We didn't. And we weren't even dating then. We were—"

"—Just friends." Maggie finished for him.

He met Maggie's eyes and felt his heart lurch. That gleam of joy was because of him. Well, at least, because of the happy memories they'd created together. "Funny," he murmured, "it doesn't seem that long ago."

"No," Maggie said softly, "it doesn't."

"But that was two years before Dad died," Zak added, almost to himself. "So." He cleared his throat. "I've come to a decision."

"Oh?"

He picked up his glass and ran a fingertip around its rim. "I, uh..."

Maggie cocked her head.

Zak shifted in his seat. "What I mean to say is that, well, there's—" He glanced away from Maggie then back to her. "I'm guessing that you're wanting to find out more about Eleanor, right?"

Maggie nodded. "I'm wanting to find out how Eleanor and the pendant are connected."

"And I'm wanting to know where the hell *Lady's Revenge* is now."

"Okay..." Maggie said.

Zak rubbed a hand across his jaw. "The pendant's tied to Eleanor. And Eleanor's tied to the wreck I'm looking for...so it makes sense for everyone if we join forces, I think."

Maggie gave an involuntary laugh. "Wait, what?"

"Just to be clear: I'm not treasure hunting, I'm uncovering evidence about the ship," he added quickly. "I was thinking that what we discover about Eleanor and the pendant will tell me more details about the fate of *Lady's Revenge,* and by extension, the ship's location now."

"This is a switch," Maggie studied him as she took a sip of her drink.

"Yeah, well..." Zak trailed off. "I read

that article you sent me. It got me thinking."

Maggie looked down as she swirled the contents of her glass then glanced back up at him. "All right," she said. "It's a deal."

Zak nodded and leaned back in his seat. "We can meet at Granddad's cottage at Dalvay tomorrow mid-morning."

Suddenly, Maggie drew in a sharp breath. "If we find out what happened to the pendant—" her eyes widened and she leaned forward "—then we'll also find out what happened to Eleanor and the ship. It must all fit together somehow."

"Mmm," Zak tugged on his earlobe. "I don't know if that's one hundred percent accurate, exactly. We don't want to go jumping to conclusions, so we'll need to formulate some theories."

"Well..." Maggie tapped her fingernail against her chin. "in that letter, Kidd said he owed Eleanor. So maybe Kidd took the pendant from her, intended to give it back, but couldn't before he, er, died?"

"That's a possibility. I mean, Kidd was in India at one point."

A gleam came into Maggie's eyes. "Your granddad said there's lost treasure here on the island. Maybe since your ancestors were searching for it, they had something to do with all this, too?"

Zak frowned. "There's not a direct connection between the treasure and our family—we were given the letter fragment. It wasn't in our family originally." Zak fiddled with his napkin. "We'll have to do some digging on all of this." The murmur of other diners mixed with the soft rustle of the breeze. "Speaking of," he added, after a moment, "have you dug any clams lately?"

Maggie glanced down at her plate then back up at Zak. She took a sip of her water and shook her head. As she did, a stray strand fell into her eyes. She brushed it away. "I haven't had time."

Was that a trace of sadness in her tone? She took the last few bites of her battered cod.

He leaned forward. "Why not?"

Maggie gave a half-laugh. "Too busy chasing success, I guess." Her hand froze on the water glass. "Wow. That blatant honesty just slipped out. Usually I'd say something that—" she bit her lip and met Zak's gaze "—would have you believing that everything was great and that I was totally fine."

She swirled the contents of the glass. "But maybe that's because we've known each other so long. It feels like I can be completely honest with you. At least, right now." She paused. "I can open up to you and," she whispered, "that's something that I've learned is really valuable... I've missed that."

She averted her gaze, her voice low. "Missed...this." She gestured to the open water, the colors glinting golden, the sea breeze and the sense of freedom. "Missed...us talking like this, you know?"

On impulse, Zak reached across the table and placed his hand on top of hers. He stroked the thin skin above her wrist with the pad of his thumb. Her eyes flutter closed.

"Oh Zak," she whispered.

His heart pounded. He imagined he could reach across the table and wrap his arms around her. She turned her palm up, so that their fingers now intertwined. A small smile flitted across his face in answer to hers. He wanted to keep her safe and tell her everything was going to be all right. Give her anything she'd ever want and—No.

Anger surged through him. What the hell was he doing?

She'd smashed his heart into a thousand pieces—twice. His stomach clenched. She'd only come back into his life by mistake. And he wasn't going to just mistakenly start to feel something for her again. He clenched his jaw. She'd made him too vulnerable before. She'd made a fool out of him, before. He wasn't going to be that stupid again.

He disentangled their clasped hands and then shoved back his chair. "I'll see you tomorrow."

Maggie's eyes flew open and a small frown line appeared between her brows. She opened her mouth, then closed it and set her jaw as she stood up too. "Right," she said in a clipped tone. "At your granddad's place."

MID-MORNING ON WEDNESDAY, Maggie pulled into the lot at Dalvay and got out. She crossed the lawn and headed for one of the cottages nestled amongst some pines.

Zak, in a pair of torn jeans and a tan T-shirt, leaned against one of the square white columns on the porch of the small bungalow.

Maggie took a deep breath and felt her heart stutter under her turquoise blouse. She was doing this for her jewelry line. For her customers. That was all.

As she walked up the porch steps, her wedge heels clicked on the wide wooden boards. She couldn't help but remember one long-ago summer morning when she'd climbed these steps. Her feet had been bare and dusted with red sand. Saltwater drops had clung to her skin...

She swallowed. Lifted her chin. This was a professional alliance. Nothing more.

"Let's get things straight." Zak's tone was distant. When he met Maggie's gaze, she couldn't help but flinch ever so slightly. Had his eyes always been that deep shade of hazel? That blend of gold and emerald?

She shook off the thought.

"This," he said, and crossed his arms, "is strictly professional. Our past history has no bearing on this. And we work together as a team. Equally."

"Of course," Maggie said as she came to a stop in front of him. "I wouldn't expect anything less."

"Oh, good, Maggie, you're here." Ian Stuart's voice floated to them. The screen door squeaked as he opened it and gestured for them to come inside.

"Make yourselves comfortable," Mr. Stuart said, as he glanced at the clock on the wall and then turned to a serving plate on a nearby table.

Maggie crossed into the house. The scent of fresh-baked banana bread wafted to her. She smiled. The last time she'd tasted that was—Her lips compressed into a thin line.

She had to get this over with. Find the pendant. Use it for inspiration. Get back to New York. She had no time for nostalgia. And no time to be affected by Zak Stuart.

She sure as hell wasn't going to stick around long enough to do anything crazy— like develop feelings for him again...

She followed Zak into the living room and sat down on the love seat. A red-and-white granny-square afghan was thrown across the back. He sank onto the matching couch across from her.

She eyed him for a second. "So." She rummaged around in her purse. "After dinner last night, I remembered something I'd found that might help us."

Zak raised his eyebrows. "I'm listening."

Her fingers closed around smooth plastic. She drew out the dry, cracked leather pouch, now in a clear protective sleeve. "This," she said as she placed it on the glass-topped coffee table, "is the—"

"—Original leather pouch that came with that gold coin," Mr. Stuart said. "Piece of banana bread?" He offered a plate of the fragrant treat in Maggie's direction.

She took a slice and then a big bite. She carefully wiped her fingers and then slid her hands into a pair of cotton preservation gloves afterward.

"Delicious. Thank you," Maggie said.

Mr. Stuart grinned. He offered Zak a piece then looked up at the clock again. "Well, it's about time for my daily walk—gotta get some fresh air. But you two stay here as long as you like. I'll be back in a bit."

"Sure, Granddad," Zak said.

"Thanks, Mr. Stuart," Maggie added. The screen door creaked as he left. Maggie continued, "There was something written on the inside. I feel like it might have to do with Eleanor and our research." She turned the bag over so that the faded writing was displayed:

Emerald queen of the North Atlantic deep.
Jewelled heart of stone that does not sleep.
An earl, a Speaker; a Captain's unheard plea;
Twenty-three cryptic pages,
Nearly All lost to a treasure's ravages.

"Hmm." Zak jumped up and strode to the window that overlooked the Gulf of St. Lawrence.

"See any connections?" Maggie said.

"Well, it's a riddle of some sort."

Maggie nodded. "I figured that part."

"Okay." Zak rubbed his jaw. "As far as connections, we break things down piece by piece. That's how we do it in the field."

"That makes sense. So the first line..."

"Emerald queen—we know that's Eleanor Webster," Zak said. His gaze slid to Maggie's.

"Right." Maggie grinned at him. "That article in *The Prince Edward Island*

Magazine confirms it."

Zak dropped his eyes to the verse and scanned the first line again. "We've also got a place—the North Atlantic."

"The North Atlantic," Maggie muttered under her breath.

"Mmm," Zak said. "Lots of battles. Lots of shipwrecks. Lots of pirates and privateers marauding along the coast..."

Maggie straightened suddenly. "Of course. In the letter fragment, Kidd mentioned that *Lady's Revenge* was sailing in the North Atlantic."

"Eleanor's ship." Zak swallowed then shook his head.

"It's a lot to take in, isn't it?" Maggie said softly.

Zak tugged at his earlobe. "Yeah." He cleared his throat. "What about the next line? *Jewelled heart of stone that does not sleep*? It could mean figuratively..."

"No. I don't think so," Maggie said. "It means literally. A piece of jewelry in the shape of a heart. Because again in the magazine piece, Eleanor herself referred to a missing pendant... *Her* pendant."

Zak shoved his hands in his pockets. "The Pendant of the Pure Hearted."

He flipped through a small notebook that he pulled out of his shirt pocket and scribbled some notes. "But the next line: an earl, a speaker, and a captain. That's pretty specific. What would that have to do with Eleanor and the pendant?"

"Hmmm," Maggie said, "And why is the word *speaker* capitalized?"

Zak tapped a finger against his chin. "They capitalized all sorts of things randomly back then."

"But these are three very specific people. Maybe the speaker was an important person?"

"You're right." Zak cocked his head. "Wait a minute." His eyes widened. "Not just an important person..." He stalked to the window again. "An earl... and a captain..."

Maggie followed him to the window.

Zak nodded to himself. "He was *the* speaker."

"What?"

"Yes." Zak said. "The Speaker of the House of Commons."

"House of Commons...over in Britain?"

"Yep."

"Okay. So the next one: *captain*," Maggie said. "Well, Eleanor was the captain of *Lady's Revenge*..."

"True," Zak said. "So maybe the plea has to do with the pendant?" He frowned and looked out the window again. The clock ticked. Maggie tapped her fingers on her leg.

"But the captain... *an unheard plea...* That's it." He snapped his fingers. "Granddad's letter fragments pointed to it. Shortly before Kidd was executed, he wrote a letter to the Speaker of the House of Commons in May of 1701. He basically pleaded for help. He also wrote a letter in April of 1700 to the Earl of Orford, and asked for his help, too. But both of them ignored his letters."

Maggie's eyes widened. "And then Kidd wrote that third letter. To uh, his crewman named Nicholas, right? Nicholas also served with Eleanor on her ship."

Zak swore under his breath. "Right."

They both stared in silence at the riddle for a moment.

Finally, Zak said, "What happened to this?" He nodded to the pouch that once held the bracelet.

"Uh," Maggie averted her gaze from his

inquisitive glance. "I, uh...er, my cat wrecked it, actually." She bit her lip.

The screen door squeaked. Mr. Stuart must be back.

"So the unheard plea was from Captain Kidd to Nicholas... But what about the last part?" she went on hastily. "*Nearly All lost to a treasure's ravages...*What do you think it refers to?"

Ian poked his head around the corner. "Likely it's referring to that deathbed confession Nicholas gave," he interjected as he came into the room.

"Deathbed confession?" Maggie said.

Mr. Stuart went over to the coffee table and started to read the verse to himself.

"Well, not exactly." Zak glanced at his grandfather then said, "Yes, when Nicholas was dying, he talked about some treasure on "an island east of Boston." But let's not get carried away." He crossed his arms. "We're not looking for treasure, we're doing research."

"But you can't deny, Zak," Mr. Stuart fixed his grandson with a look, "that this pouch," he pointed a finger at it, "originally held the gold coin your great-great-grandfather Samuel received from John

MacDonald, one of Thomas Jefferson Beale's treasure hunting partners."

"The gold coin that became part of the antique bracelet," Maggie whispered, as her eyes widened. "But who was John?" She turned to Zak.

"Mmm." Zak rubbed the back of his neck and murmured. "John MacDonald was Nicholas's grandson. And Nicholas was Kidd's crewman and then Eleanor's..."

"You don't like the fact that this could really *be* something, do you?" Maggie crossed her arms and fixed him with a level gaze.

Zak hunched his shoulders.

"I'm sorry," Maggie said. "That wasn't very professional."

Zak cleared his throat. "But we skipped a part." He turned his attention back to the riddle. "The first part of the last line: *Twenty-three cryptic pages...*"

"More specifics," Maggie murmured. "*Cryptic...*" She frowned. "That could mean mysterious. Or it could mean encoded. What would be twenty-three pages long *and* either mysterious or encoded?"

"I can think of one thing," Ian said. "The Beale Papers."

"Except," Zak said, "there were only three pages of the Beale Papers that were encrypted." He paused. "But those three encrypted pages are supposed to reveal a treasure buried in Virginia, not on Prince Edward Island." Zak glanced at Maggie. Did he remember that she could still recall the stories he'd once shared with her, beside crackling beach bonfire, about his family connection to the papers?

She nodded at him. "Right. The rest wasn't encrypted."

"Nope, it wasn't. It was written in plain English." Zak's gaze slid to Maggie's and she saw the approval in his eyes. She felt her cheeks flush.

Then Maggie gasped. "And the whole thing *was* twenty-three pages long."

"But remember: a part of the treasure buried in Virginia was, according to John, partially Kidd's. And they did mention there was more of it out there." Ian interjected.

"Down through the years," he added, "I've done a bit of reading on Thomas Jefferson Beale. I'd always heard," he said, "that Beale was a Mason. So was your great-great grandfather, you know," Ian said and glanced at Zak with a note of pride in his voice.

Zak shifted his weight.

Ian cleared his throat. "Beale loved to create puzzles and encryptions. Like how he did with that innkeeper. So he must have written this riddle, too. Which means he probably made the pouch to conceal it, as well..."

"That makes sense," Maggie said.

"I bet Beale heard about Eleanor from John, since John probably listened to stories from his grandfather Nicholas." Zak added. He stood up and blew out a sharp breath. "Which means *Lady's Revenge*, the pendant and this possible supposed treasure *are* connected. So." Zak steepled his fingers and sat down on the couch. "In order to continue gathering evidence for our research, we need to look at—"

"—The Beale Papers," Maggie and Zak said in unison.

Gulls called outside the window, and the occasional car rumbled by on the road. "Well, let's go." Maggie said to Zak.

"I'd say you could look at the Beale Papers online right here," Ian said, "but with the riddle being that old, it'd be smart to look at the originals." He threw Zak a pointed glance. Zak shifted in his seat. Tugged at his earlobe.

Maggie watched Zak. "You know where the papers are?" She got up and began to walk to the door. "Let's go get them."

Zak stayed seated. Maggie's steps slowed. She glanced back at Zak with her brows lifted.

"The original Beale Papers are at Eddie's place now," Zak said.

Maggie winced. "Not your half-crazy uncle's?"

"Unfortunately, yes."

Chapter Five

LATER WEDNESDAY EVENING, Maggie sat at the desk in her hotel room. Tried to ignore the blank sketchpad that sat beside her.

Her phone buzzed and she glanced at it. Nicky had sent a text: *Great news! The* Sun *just called. They were looking for you. I told them you weren't available but they really wanted to write up a piece about you and the new project, so I told them all about it.*

Maggie chewed her lip as she texted back: *Good work!* She didn't have to worry. This was about her new piece, not the bracelet. That would help create some more publicity for her brand and for the new piece when it came out. She tapped the pencil idly against her chin. Just then, her phone rang.

"Hi Maggie." Her stomach churned at

the sound of Jia's voice. "What do you have for us?"

"I..." She swallowed. She couldn't lie to Courtney Jewelers. "I'm still working on things," she said at last.

Jia laughed. "Not avoiding us, are you?"

"Of course not." Maggie said, too quickly.

"Good," Jia said. "Unfortunately, if you don't meet the deadline, we're going to find someone else this time. We need something by the start of the day Friday."

Maggie's palms began to sweat. "Yes, of course. I'll have something right away."

"Great," Jia said, voice cheery. "We look forward to reviewing it."

Maggie ended the call.

She took the pencil and closed her eyes. The pencil lead, freshly sharpened, pressed against the page and seemed to cut into it. Deep. As if it were breaking in two. Breaking apart. Breaking into a million pieces.

Like a shattered heart. Perhaps that had been how Eleanor had felt when she'd lost the pendant.

Maggie sucked in a breath. Felt the hairs on the back of her neck stand up. All at once, her pencil began to move along the page. Slowly at first, but then gaining more speed as she gave in to her emotions.

All those days and nights spent alone after she'd left Zak. Too afraid to really face her own lies and the deeper truth within her heart when she looked at him, looked into his heart.

She felt a sob build in her chest but she didn't stifle it like she'd done so many times before.

Her pencil continued to move, almost of its own volition. She fed every tiny piece of herself and her jagged, pent-up feelings down through the pencil and out onto the page.

The lines blurred as she blinked.

Blurred and seemed to take on a new shape, a new form even as she continued to sketch.

At last, she put the pencil down and took a slow, deep breath. Her eyes closed and she sat still. Felt the rhythm of her heart rate begin to slow.

In. Out. She took another deep breath as she slowly opened her eyes and looked down at the page.

She blinked once. Twice. The image on

the page came into focus.

Beautiful and tragic were the first words that came to mind as she gazed at it. As if the heart had only now begun to bleed for what was left behind. Just like Eleanor, in a way... What deeper tragedies had Eleanor experienced?

Maggie pursed her lips. This design was pretty much the exact opposite of the bracelet. But her customers would surely love it? She knew they'd love the romantic story of Eleanor that she'd begun to uncover.

Yes. This would be perfect. She took a picture of it with her phone and then emailed it to Jia.

She sat back and slowly exhaled.

So was this it, then? She chewed her lip and her stomach dipped. Now that she'd completed her submission, she could just go home, back to Pierniki, to her apartment and...

But no. She hadn't found out all she could about Eleanor. And it'd been so satisfying, discovering the secrets behind the riddle. She couldn't stop now. She had to find out exactly how Eleanor and the pendant were connected. It would be more background for her jewelry line. Besides, as someone who had experienced a broken heart, Maggie felt, in a way, that she owed it to Eleanor to find out the rest of her story.

Not only that, Zak had said he wanted to help her. She couldn't just walk away—again. He needed her help. And she needed to help him.

So she'd stay.

THE NEXT MORNING, Zak shut the driver's door of his pickup as Maggie, in a pair of jeans and an aqua-colored T-shirt, climbed up into the cab beside him.

He merged onto the TransCanada highway and headed down east to Eddie's place.

He reached over to the dash to flick on the radio and his fingers collided with Maggie's. A jolt passed through him. "Old habits die hard?" But Maggie was a habit he couldn't quite break.

Why was he even thinking this? Was he trying to test his limits? Purposely make himself angry at her?

No, a small voice inside said, he was trying to push her away. Push away the old feelings he thought he'd buried. Push away any trace of vulnerability that might show in his eyes. He couldn't risk Maggie thinking she'd gotten to him.

Maggie glanced at him and smoothed down the non-existent wrinkles in her T-shirt. "Something like that. Looks like we both still can't stand silence in the car." She fiddled with the hem of her top. "Where's your uncle's, again?"

But the radio announcer came on before Zak could reply. *"The first of the monster storms hit the New England coast yesterday, which caused millions of dollars in damage. Crops in the area have been decimated. The storms are expected to hit hard as they work their way up the Eastern Seaboard toward Canada."*

"Damn it," Zak said. His hands tightened on the wheel.

"Not good for your dives if the storms come up this far, is it?" Maggie said.

Zak shook his head. "Nope." He slid a glance toward Maggie. "I really thought I'd figure out the location of the wreck by now..." He felt something loosen in his chest. It felt good to unburden himself to her. No, not her specifically. Just another person. She was merely a listening ear. "I combed Davies' journal and rechecked all my calculations."

"Maybe you're thinking too hard," Maggie said.

"Maybe I am." He paused. Glanced at her. "But thanks to that article you found, I've looked up *The Patagonia's* logbooks. What was left of them. I *think* I've got some possible new coordinates to try out along the South Shore here. But if a storm hits like it's predicted to, it won't be safe to dive. Even if it was, sand and debris would get kicked up from the shifting currents and make it hard to see."

Zak pursed his lips. "I need to find it," he muttered as he shoved his free hand through his hair.

"I'm sure you'll think of something. You always have before."

"Well, thanks." Warmth curled through his chest. No. He clenched his jaw. She was just being nice. Just saying that. He swallowed. "We're almost there."

"Hopefully," Maggie added, "Eddie'll be having one of his good days."

The wind picked up as Zak pulled the truck onto a long rutted red-dirt driveway. He darted a glance at Maggie. But if she remembered another, similar dirt road they'd gone down that one summer evening, she didn't give any indication.

He shook off the thought and steered the Dodge around a sharp curve then came to a stop amid long grass and gnarled oak and maple trees. He got out.

But when Maggie's door slammed behind him, he paused mid-stride as a jolt of memory passed through him. That one summer evening, her passenger door had slammed just like that—He shook off the memory.

A dog barked.

He felt Maggie next to him as he started up the path that led to the small postwar house. Paint peeled from the narrow eaves. The porch roof sagged ever so slightly. That old lighthouse had been ramshackle like this, too, Zak couldn't help but recall.

Zak frowned at himself as he walked up the front steps and went into the enclosed sun porch. He noticed a shaft of sunlight that beamed through a smudged, dirty window. The dust motes danced on the sunbeam, just like they had inside the lighthouse on that summer evening...

Zak got out of his silver Honda. The early evening light spilled across the bright yellow of the canola field. Maggie slammed the passenger door behind him. The breeze carried the scent of fresh-cut hay.

She came to stand beside him as he looked up at the cherry-red trim around the windows and door of the three-story white clapboard lighthouse.

"So they actually put a road in to this place?" she asked.

Zak nodded. "A few years ago. Not much of a road, really. More like a rutted track. But it serves its purpose." He stared at her a minute.

"Thanks again for coming back to the island to help me and Mom and Dad with loading all their stuff into that U-Haul. I know you have so much to do now that you've finished your doctorate and got that job at Memorial."

"Hey, what are long-distance boyfriends for?" Zak teased, and kissed the top of her head. "Of course. I was happy to help, Maggie. You mean a lot to me."

She smiled at him but it faltered and she

quickly averted her gaze. "They're really looking forward to retirement in warmer temperatures." She cleared her throat. "God, the last time we were out here was high school graduation night," she said as she threw a glance over her shoulder at him.

Zak studied her. "I remember." That night, she'd broken up with him. Said she'd decided to go to college in New York while he'd stayed here and gone to UPEI for his undergrad. But that was in the past. They'd started dating again, long-distance, a little more than year ago, while he finished up his PhD.

"Do they still call it the secret lighthouse?"

He nodded. Grinned. "And the door's still unlocked."

Maggie headed around the opposite side of the structure. The yellow blooms of canola brushed against her denim capris.

And all at once, he was far too aware of the swing of her hips as she climbed the two steps to the door. She pushed it open—its paint peeled, its weathered boards warped. A stark contrast to the bright new coat of paint on its octagonal sides.

The musty smell of dusty neglect hit him

as she headed for the far corner behind the set of stairs.

Maggie reached a hand out and traced their initials inside a heart scrawled with Bic pen. A half-smile lifted her lips for a fraction of a second. "We were only together for our last year in high school weren't we? Seems like a hundred years ago." She swallowed, blinked back tears.

"I know," he said, so close his breath tickled her ear.

She tensed, as if she wanted to jump, pull away.

"Want to see if the view from the top's still the same?"

Maggie must have heard the knowing smile in his voice. She blushed. Turned away. "Sure."

Zak gestured to the stairs. "Ladies first." His gaze locked with hers.

She put a hand on the almost-vertical rail of the staircase. "If I fall, I know I'll have somewhere soft to land."

He raised his eyebrows.

She started to climb.

Flies droned amid dusty cobwebs at the window she passed. She stepped out onto the first story platform. The walls slanted slightly

inward as she stood and waited for him to climb to her level.

She glanced up. Two more stories.

The next ladder was even steeper, and she gripped the handrail a bit more tightly as it wobbled under their combined weight. He saw her swallow but she kept climbing. They stepped out onto the final platform together.

Both of them stooped slightly as the walls narrowed even more on the third floor. The tiny space seemed airless, as if it floated on the tides of memory.

Zak looked out the small pane of glass.

Above their heads, the fixture for the heavy glass lighthouse beacon had rusted into place. The grate, which let the heat from the kerosene out, now let dusky twilight filter in over both of them.

"Think that'll hold us?" Zak gestured to a small crawlspace, open to the elements, that led to a railed walkway.

Without a second thought, Maggie dropped to her knees and crawled out onto the walkway. Then she straightened and leaned against the rail.

Zak joined her at the rail. Put one arm so that it rested deliberately casually against the rail. And the other...his heart jumped...was around her on the other side. When had that happened?

"Remember this?" he murmured, with his lips next to her ear. His breath stirred the dark strands around the nape of her neck and she shivered. He saw goose bumps rise on her bare arms. She swallowed. He remembered that evening all too well...

How the starlight had reflected in her eyes. The long mournful call of the foghorn. The warmth of her cotton shirt as she'd curled her fingers around his. How he'd wrapped his arms around her and pulled her close.

Memory and reality collided as Zak realized he had done the exact same thing again.

Maggie stared up at him, her lips parted, as he watched her.

The breeze ruffled his hair, still a shade too long. She reached up and smoothed a strand across his forehead.

She leaned into his warmth. As if she was letting it surround her.

His arms tightened around her waist.

"How can you be so sure?" she said, her lips inches from his. "About us now that we've gotten back together again?"

"Because, deep down, I always have

been," he replied. He tucked a strand of wind-blown hair behind her ear. "And," he whispered, "I always will be."

Zak reached up and traced a finger along the outline of her lips. "Shhh," he said as she started to open her mouth to protest. "It's okay. I forgive you." He moved his caress to her cheek, and she licked her lips. Swallowed hard. "But I was so awful to you. I-I broke your heart. And now you're offering it up again to me on a silver platter?"

Zak chuckled. "I wouldn't say a silver platter exactly. More like a slightly scarred cutting board."

Maggie buried her face in his shirt and mumbled, "You know what I mean."

"Hey, there's nothing to forgive," Zak whispered. "Things happen. Time heals. Besides, we've been dating for over a year now. My heart has had plenty of time to decide that—"

"Don't do this," Maggie said, her voice sharp. "You can't just play the martyr and say everything's all right when it's not. You can't just throw your heart fully into this again and expect me to pick it up and put it on a shelf somewhere safe." Her jaw clenched. "How can you give yourself away so *easily?"*

Zak sighed and suddenly felt old. "When I was dating other people, I only thought about you. And I guess... I guess," he tucked his chin into his chest, and a strand of hair fell across his forehead again. "I want you to know that 'us' feels so real and true that I'm willing to give it my all." He captured her fingers in his. "Willing to go all in." Zak traced the veins on the back of Maggie's hand. "And maybe," he said, as he met her gaze, "it will all be worth it. Because I love you."

He dropped to one knee.

The bark and growl of a dog behind the screen door jerked Zak back to the present.

The dog growled again, low in its throat, and launched itself at the screen door. As the screen door burst open, Zak threw himself in front of Maggie.

Before the dog could lunge onto Zak, a deep voice boomed, "Carl!" The dog immediately stopped and turned back toward the voice.

Floorboards creaked. A rail-thin man in a bright orange baseball cap with grease spots stood in the shadow of the doorway. He held a 12-gauge shotgun.

"How the hell are ya, Zak? Gone and got yourself married, then, did ya?"

Maggie saw Zak shift his weight away from her. She took a deep breath to calm the flutter of her heart. He was just protecting her from danger. Anyone would've done the same in his position.

Zak cleared his throat. Rubbed at his elbow in a gesture she recognized as discomfort.

"God, no," she answered for him. "We're not married." But for a second, she remembered that one summer evening...

She looked at him, down on one knee, there in the golden evening light. Her heart squeezed and she felt like she might throw up.

"Will you marry me?" he asked.

She had to stop this. Had to stop it now before it got any worse. A knife of guilt and shame twisted in her gut. He'd been unfair to her when he'd asked her to stay on the island and go to college here instead of in New York. And now? They were in different places in their lives, in their careers. If she said yes, she'd be treating him unfairly. It wouldn't be fair to the marriage, either. It would be like they weren't even married if they weren't living in the same place...

Her chin trembled. She couldn't just walk away from her career in New York, not after she'd put so much time and effort into it. Sure, none of the jewelry companies were buying her designs, but that was bound to change. It had to. And she couldn't let him give up this great job opportunity at Memorial, either. His career was too important to him, too. They'd talked about that so many times...

She needed to set him free. She couldn't love him like this. He should be with someone else. Someone who had time to be with him, to live where he lived.

All her hesitation, all her hanging back, she couldn't ignore it any more. She had to follow her own heart and let him go. So they could be free to go in the directions they both needed to now.

"I know you've put your heart on the line here. I know you've opened up to me, let me in, shown me all your secret hiding places. And that's very sweet of you."

"Then say yes," he whispered. His eyes held hers.

She looked at him without blinking as she disentangled her fingers from his. She took a step back, her heart lighter but her shoulders tense as she studied his expression.

He swallowed and blinked rapidly.

"Don't cry," she whispered, "please don't cry. I just...I don't love you."

Zak crossed his arms.

"Why the hell not?" Eddie shoved the brim of his ball cap up with the shotgun barrel. "You're perfect for each other."

Zak shifted his weight. "I didn't realize you got a dog, Eddie."

The old man shrugged his thin shoulders. "Can never be too careful in these parts. Government cover-ups all over out here. Last week I saw a tube ship fly by—glowing red. Weird as hell. Hours later, a cluster of men in all-black suits show up at my door 'n tell me I've seen nothin' 'n can tell no one."

"But you just did," Zak said.

Eddie shrugged. "You're family, Zak. I know you won't say anything." He grinned, and Maggie saw a gold tooth flash.

"Well," Zak said, "we're not UFO hunting today."

"We're looking for some documents," Maggie added.

A gleam came into Eddie's eyes. "So

you've finally decided to believe the tales, boy?"

Maggie answered for him again. "We're just..."

The old man burst into laughter. "Sure, tell yourselves whichever ya like." He leaned the shotgun against the doorframe, raised a stiff, arthritic hand, and gestured for them to come inside.

The scent of chocolate chip cookies wafted to Maggie. "Have a seat." Eddie waved a hand at a dusty green velvet Victorian settee. "Don't mind my filing system. You can move that." He nodded at Zak. "Just working on my memoir."

An old Remington typewriter balanced on one corner of the faded couch. A neatly typed page protruded from it.

Maggie leaned down and picked up an old empty Rice Krispies cereal box stuffed with more typed pages. She looked around for a place on the floor to set it, but only saw more boxes and piles of trinkets.

She carefully set down the cereal box. Zak swept off the thick layer of dust before he took a seat. The springs creaked under him. Maggie carefully sat beside him. The settee wobbled slightly.

Eddie reappeared with a plate of cookies. "I just bake for something to do. How many cookies do youse want?" He patted his round belly. "They came fresh from the oven."

"What's with your family and baking?" Maggie muttered around a mouthful of cookie.

Zak shrugged. He took a cookie.

Eddie took two and dunked them in his coffee. He sat down across from them on a weathered church pew.

Zak leaned forward, his tone serious. "Eddie, we need to look at the Beale Papers. It's kind of time sensitive."

Maggie couldn't help but smile. The faintest trace of Maritime accent had crept back into Zak's voice as he spoke to Eddie.

Eddie scratched his head. "'Fraid that's not possible."

"What do you mean?" Maggie's fingers gripped the soft velvet fabric.

"Sold 'em." Eddie propped his feet up on a small wooden chest about the size of a microwave. Its top was slightly rounded and it had wide bands of metal that ran vertically up the sides and across the top.

Maggie noticed its leather handles had

partially been eaten away by either mice or seawater. Or possibly both.

"You sold them?" Zak's eyes widened. "But those are part of our family history. Great-Great-Granddad wrote them."

"So now you decide to care?" Eddie's voice held no trace of bitterness, though. He sounded more amused than anything.

Zak said nothing.

"I needed the money," Eddie sighed. Gave Zak a sidelong look. "Bank was gonna foreclose on my property here. You know how money gets tight on the island in winter. I didn't qualify for Employment Insurance last few years."

Maggie saw Zak's knuckles whiten as his hands tightened into fists at his sides. He stood abruptly.

Maggie followed suit. "Well, thanks for the cookies anyway, Eddie," she said.

"Any time, any time. You come by and visit again soon, will ya?"

"Sure," Zak called without looking back. Maggie saw the tension in his shoulders.

Zak was just about to the screen door when Eddie suddenly jumped up. The dog, who'd gone to sleep on the porch, snapped to attention and began to bark again.

"Carl!" Eddie shouted. The dog fell silent. "The Voynich manuscript. Sold a rare medieval copy of *that*. Made a pretty penny on it, too." He grinned. "Nope, nope."

Zak turned slowly around. Maggie took a deep steadying breath.

"Still got 'em..." A twinkle came into Eddie's eyes. "Just wanted to make sure you were serious about our family's heritage, Zak." He slapped Zak on the shoulder. "No hard feelings, eh?"

Zak muttered something under his breath that Maggie couldn't hear.

"So," Eddie continued, "they're around here...somewhere." He gestured to the living room, which was a maze of piled boxes, filing cabinets and enough furniture to stock an antique store.

Maggie's heart fell to her shoes.

The old man stared into space for a minute, his head cocked, a frown on his face. Suddenly he closed his eyes. Inhaled then exhaled slowly three times. "Now," he said to himself, "where would they be?" He passed a hand over his closed eyes.

"He does this every time he loses

something," Zak whispered in Maggie's ear. "Says it helps him clear his mind and remember."

"Why," Maggie whispered, "does Eddie even *have* the Beale Papers? They should be in a museum."

Zak lips twitched. "Let's just say my dad lost a bet with Eddie years ago."

Maggie felt a shiver slide down her spine as Zak's warm breath caressed her cheek.

The minutes ticked by. The only sound was the occasional thump of the dog's tail and the sudden loud call of the cuckoo clock in the corner. Maggie jumped at the sound.

Eddie's eyes snapped open. "Of course," he muttered to himself. Then he grinned over at Zak and Maggie and tapped his temple. "Best filing system is up here."

He pointed a gnarled finger down at the floor in front of him. "The Beale Papers are right here. In my safest filing system to date." He chuckled and started to crouch down in front of the battered wooden box. But the old man suddenly stopped, an expression of pain on his face.

Zak rushed over. "Uncle Eddie," He

placed a hand on Eddie's shoulder. "Here, let me do that. I know how your arthritis acts up."

Eddie sighed and lifted his eyes to Zak. "Mighty kind of ya, Zak—always were a good 'un." Zak helped Eddie to the more comfortable stuffed wingback near the couch. The old man nodded in the direction of the worn, beat-up box. Eddie chuckled. "No one would think of looking in that rust bucket."

"Where did you get it anyway, Eddie?" Maggie said.

"Funny thing, that." Eddie scratched the back of his neck. "Went out 'n bought myself a metal detector way back. Very first day I had it I was bound and deter-mined to strike it rich." He paused. "Was on a beach near here no one goes to, low tide; sure enough, she started makin' a crackly noise and flashed all sorts of lights at me. I got my shovel out." He grinned and his gold tooth flashed.

"But I didn't hardly needed it, 'cause the top corner was pokin' just at the surface. Well, I cleared away the rest of the sand and uncovered this here chest. No gold inside—it was completely empty. But

I kept it as a souvenir of my first find. Good for storing papers and that." He paused. "Did ya see the initials on the front?" He nodded at the rusted keyhole. "*J. F.* Also noticed somethin' odd with it. Scorch marks—you can still see 'em if you look." He shrugged. "Maybe someone tried to get rid of it. Threw it overboard. And it washed ashore."

Maggie's eyes widened. "Wow."

"Tell you what," Eddie said. "After you look in there, you can keep it. I've seen how you were eyeing it, Maggie. Well, take it. It's yours."

MAGGIE PEERED INSIDE the old sea chest. Scraps of watered silk, stained and ragged-edged, were piled on top of wallpaper samples, all thrown haphazardly into the shrunken wooden tray that acted as a shelf in the chest.

Maggie reached in and helped Zak remove the scraps of fabric and paper. But as they sifted through the material to the bottom, they found nothing.

Zak lifted the small wooden tray out

and set it down on the floor.

A pile of yellowed newspapers lay underneath. Mustiness wafted to Maggie as she glanced at the date—1892.

Eddie grinned. "Had to have a place to stick 'em. Never know when you might need somethin'."

Maggie carefully lifted out the yellowed pages. Underneath there was a leather pouch about the size of a letter. Her breath caught.

Zak rummaged around in his jeans pocket and pulled out a pair of wrinkled white cotton gloves.

"Like a boy scout, aren't you?" Maggie couldn't help teasing him.

"Never hurts," Zak said, a glint in his eye that Maggie couldn't quite read.

"So," she said to cover up the swoop in her stomach, "let's have a look."

She watched Zak's long, strong fingers close around the old leather. He met Maggie's gaze. "Here," he said, his hazel eyes serious, "you open it."

Maggie's heart skipped a beat as he handed her the gloves.

She slipped them on then reached out and began to unwind the strap that wound around the leather pouch.

After the last of the binding fell away, a sheaf of neatly stacked, though yellowed and brittle, pages was revealed. Zak stood. So did Maggie. He strode over to the kitchen table and placed the leather pouch on the neatly pressed and spotless tablecloth.

Eddie followed behind.

Zak put the pages on the table.

"You know," Maggie said, "since the riddle said twenty-three cryptic pages, maybe it'd be useful to lay each page out side by side just so we can pick up on any patterns or anything."

"Good idea," Zak said. He put action to Maggie's words.

Maggie helped him. The faded ink and swooping, curled letters of each line made Maggie smile. She leaned forward to examine the text.

They scanned the first few pages in silence. "I don't see anything here—" Zak began.

"Wait a minute." Maggie cocked her head and narrowed her eyes. "What's that?"

"What?" Zak said.

Maggie pointed to the very first line. "That capital letter *T*." She tapped a finger on the page. "There's two lines…"

Zak frowned. "You're right," he said. "They both start beside the *T*. It forms what basically looks like a greater-than sign beside the *T*."

T >

"That has to be what *cryptic* meant in the riddle." Maggie felt her heart speed up. Could this actually be real? The evidence, it seemed, was staring her right in the face.

"So," Zak said, "we have to look for more letters with marks somewhere around them…"

They scanned the rest of the page in silence. "I don't see anything else."

"Well, since it said twenty-three pages, maybe there's just one per page?"

"Good thinking," Zak said.

"But," Eddie interjected, "there are twenty-six letters in the alphabet."

"True," Zak said.

"Look," Maggie said. "There's another one. But it's not the first line and first capital letter. It varies. Whoever did this wanted to be as subtle as possible."

They searched each page. Maggie had pulled a pad of neon pink Post-Its from her purse and began to write down each letter they discovered.

After reaching twenty-three, she frowned. "The last page must have...three letters."

"You're right," Zak said. "Here's *X*."

"There's *Y*," Maggie pointed to a sentence a third of the way down.

"And there's *Z*," Eddie said, a note of triumph in his voice.

Maggie continued to jot down the letters on the sticky note. "Okay. Here's what I've found."

She showed Zak the pad.

He frowned. "That looks just like a jumble of strangely marked letters."

"Until," Maggie said, "you rearrange them." She took a clean sticky note and began rearranging the letters. "If my hunch is right about this, it'll form a grid."

"Still love codes and puzzles, looks like," Zak said, his voice low in her ear.

Maggie's breath caught. "I do the *New York Times* crossword every day. And," she managed, "the crypt-o-quote." She forced herself to meet his direct gaze.

"That's impressive," Zak said.

"Keeps my mind sharp," she replied.

"Now," she said, "judging from my rearrangement of letters, it looks like this is a pigpen cipher key." She held up the Post-It. "See?"

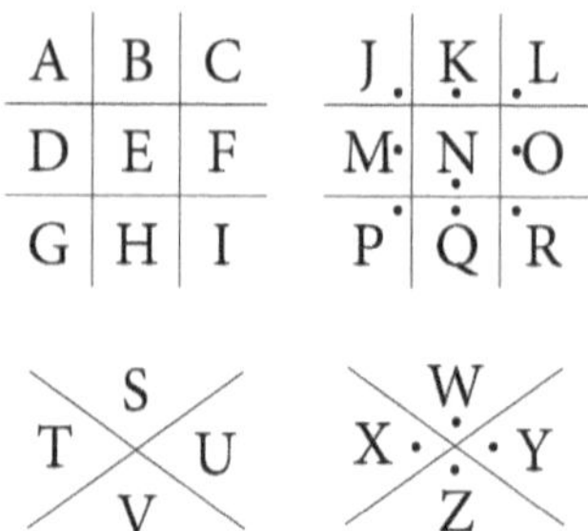

"A pigpen what?" Zak's brows furrowed.

"The pigpen cipher was used by the Masons to encode their documents," Maggie explained. "Also known as the Masonic cipher or tic-tac-toe cipher. It's a simple substitution cipher."

"Okay," Zak said. He tapped his fingers against the tabletop. "So... this cipher key must have been written by my great-great grandfather, since he's the one who wrote the Beale Papers." He chuckled and glanced at Eddie. "Beale must have sworn

Samuel to secrecy, because I never heard anything about this pigpen cipher key from any of my relatives. Did you?"

Eddie shook his head.

Maggie's eyes widened. "Ian did say they were both Masons, so Beale and Samuel must've made some sort of secret agreement about the whole thing." She waved a hand at the Post-It. "The grid exchanges letters for symbols. Take away these letters here—" she tapped a finger on the neon pink sticky note "—and you have just the symbols." She drew lines on another Post-It. "For example, the symbol for *T* would be that greater-than sign. *C* uses two lines like a right angle for its symbol. *Q* uses a square without a bottom and a dot at the top for its symbol, and so on. Like this."

"So." Maggie took a breath. "Since these grids include letters, not just the symbols with lines and dots, this is a pigpen cipher key."

"A key to what?" Zak frowned and looked out the window.

"A secret message written in some other document," Maggie said.

"I can't resist—" Zak said, as he met her gaze.

Maggie's pulse thudded. For a second, she imagined he was going to say "you."

"—asking why it's called a pigpen cipher?" Zak's lips quirked upward.

Maggie fought a nudge of disappointment in her stomach then grinned back at him. "The lines look a bit like pens. And the dots could be pigs."

They shared a laugh.

"So." Zak cleared his throat. He got up and headed to the window. Scraped a hand across his stubble. "We need to figure out which document this is referring to."

"Well," Maggie said, "based on the riddle, the document, or documents, must have something to do with either Kidd or Eleanor."

The cuckoo clock chimed in the living room.

"Wait a second." Zak shoved his hands into his pockets then pulled them out again and ran a hand through his hair. "*An earl, a Speaker; a Captain's unheard plea...*"

Maggie raised her eyebrows. "What are

you not saying?"

"Captain Kidd's *unheard plea*," Zak said. "His letters to the Speaker of the House of Commons and the Earl of Orford—I have scans of the originals."

"Then what are we waiting for?" Maggie neatly stacked the Beale Papers, along with the other odds and ends that had been in the chest, and handed them to Eddie. "Thank you so much. This chest is great, and your help has been, too," she said, as she picked up the chest and then turned to Zak. "We have to take a look at those letters."

Chapter Six

"KIDD'S LETTERS SHOULD be in here somewhere," Zak said, more for something to say—and to hide his awareness of Maggie—than because he needed to explain.

"Right," Maggie said.

Zak slid a key into the lock in the drawer of a gray metal desk. He tensed, careful to avoid bumping into Maggie, who stood less than a foot away. As he pulled open the drawer, birds chirped outside the half-open living room window of his rented house.

His heart ached as he looked at her face in profile. Her brow was smooth, and she stared out the window at the calm water of the bay. She seemed so unconcerned.

His jaw clenched.

Despite that, he handled each document and artifact gently. His breath caught in his throat as he sensed Maggie's eyes on him.

"I got scans of these when I went to the Historical Manuscripts Commission over in England," Zak said. "They keep pretty much everything." He chuckled even though it wasn't really a joke. Why was he rambling? He mentally shook his head. "After I helped find that wreck of Kidd's, it's amazing who wants to give you grant money for other, similar projects."

"Right," Maggie said again.

What was he doing? Trying to impress her? Of course not. "Okay," he said, "they're in here."

He pulled out a red file folder and opened it. "Yep. Right on top." He picked up the two sheets. "Kidd was pretty desperate when he wrote these, you know. Edward Russell, the Earl of Orford, who was basically his boss, wasn't known for being a nice person." Zak glanced at Maggie. "Kidd wrote the second letter three days after he was sentenced to death."

Maggie leaned toward him. She still used that honeysuckle-and-vanilla body lotion? He'd gotten her that for Christmas

one year—He cleared his throat. "If you read the last lines on the second letter, Kidd's basically warning other seamen to be wary of people in authority."

"Good advice," Maggie said as she glanced at Zak then down at the folder. "So let's take a look at both of these side by side." She picked up the letters and placed them on the desk top, seemingly unaware of her affect on him. "To further confuse people, this pigpen cipher may be arranged across both letters, since it's an easy cipher to break if you have the key."

"If it's so easy, why did they use it?"

Maggie shrugged. "Human nature. Even though this was done something like three hundred years ago, some things don't change. They wanted something quick and easy. Probably wanted to spend more time digging up gold bars on the beach than deciphering complex clues."

Zak nodded. He picked up the first letter and began to read it.

"I say that, but..." Maggie frowned. "It looks like there's nothing actually written on here."

"These *are* scans of the originals. If it's on here, we'll find it." Zak's tone was more fierce than he intended.

"Hmm." Maggie set down the letter she was studying. She tapped a fingernail against the paper. The bare bulb overhead swayed gently back and forth in the light breeze from the opened window.

He tried to ignore the way the wind flirted with strands of her hair that brushed against her skin and... He couldn't afford to daydream or romanticize her or his old feelings for her. It had led to nothing but heartache. And would lead to the same again. He forced his eyes back to the page. "What about this?" He pointed to the second letter, which was dated 1701. "There's ink spots and quill pen drag marks down at the bottom here."

"Mmm." Her brow furrowed in con-centration as she studied the piece of paper. Her head jerked up suddenly. "What if I was wrong?" she whispered and looked straight at him.

"Come on, Maggie. Don't doubt your-self like that. I know that ninety-nine times out of one hundred, you're usually right—" he winced. "Sorry, I didn't mean—"

"It's okay." She waved a hand in his direction. "We have more important things to fight about now than that." The corners

of her lips quirked upward.

His own mouth lifted in response.

They looked at each other. Seconds ticked by. One minute. Two. Zak felt himself hold his breath. Then exhale. Shook his head. He didn't have time for this.

He returned his attention to the letter.

MAGGIE LEANED CLOSER to Zak and traced a fingertip along the markings underneath some of the sentences and paragraphs of the second letter. "Ink spots," she murmured. "No, those aren't ink spots." She cocked her head. "They look more deliberate than that...Yes. *That's* the pigpen cipher." She scrambled for the tablet of paper nearby then picked up her pen. "They've disguised the cipher around ink spots to confuse the casual observer."

"So what are we looking for?" Zak asked.

Maggie made a few quick strokes on the tablet of paper then held it up for him. "Anything that might resemble these kinds of markings."

<   ^   >

"You remember," she continued, "what the pigpen cipher key looks like, right? So we want as many of those same type of markings as possible. Some of the marks will have dots beside or around them, too. Although they're gonna look less distinct than what I've done with a ballpoint pen. Here," she said, "check the other letter."

Zak took the scanned page from her and began to skim it. "There aren't any on here." He looked over the page again. "Definitely nothing."

Maggie didn't reply. She continued to jot down the marks, dots and lines from the second letter until the entire page of the yellow legal pad was covered.

Just as Zak was about to open his mouth to comment, Maggie looked up. "Now we apply the key and figure out what this is."

Her cheeks were flushed and her eyes sparkled.

"Right," he managed. He studied the page. Despite himself, answering excitement washed through him. This could be leading to something...big.

He felt the heat of her nearness and imagined it felt very much like the heat of his own blood.

And the sparkle in her eye must have matched a sparkle in his own because she grinned at him like she could read his thoughts.

"The key." He cleared his throat and pulled it out of the file marked *Bay Fortune.*

He picked up a pen and began to help her to decipher the marks. Minutes ticked by in silence until he said, "I think I have something." He began to read. "*Lines of love/Locked in—*"

Maggie's voice sounded soft in his ear as she picked up the rest of the phrase. "*—a prison of glass/Where—*" She stopped reading. "That can't be the whole message," she said as she picked up the letters and checked them thoroughly again. "But there is nothing more here."

She chewed on her lip, glanced at Zak and then looked away. Was that disappointment in her eyes?

"Well," he said, "we need to figure out what this part of the riddle means."

"Maybe then we'll know where to look for the rest? And then be able to figure out where Eleanor's pendant is."

"And the ship." Zak cleared his throat. "So. *Lines of love.*" He cocked his head.

Maggie twirled a strand of hair around her finger. "It was back in the days of sailing ships. Maybe lines means ropes?"

"That doesn't make any sense."

"No, you're right. It doesn't," Maggie said.

"Okay, so what else could lines be referring to?"

"Well, lines are usually straight. Narrow." Maggie chewed on the strand of her hair. "Parallel to each other..."

"But then there's the 'of love' part. So I don't think we're talking about literal lines."

"But this is a riddle," Maggie countered.

"Written by pirates," Zak replied.

"True."

"What do lines and love have to do with each other?" Zak's brow furrowed.

"Well, there's always Shakespeare."

Zak arched a brow.

Maggie grinned. "I miss this," she said all at once.

The smile slipped off Zak's face. "I know," he replied.

Maggie tucked a stray strand of her hair behind her ear and ducked her head.

"*Lines of love*," he muttered.

"Lines, dots, dashes." Maggie said. "Wait a minute. What do you make lines with?"

"Rulers? Pencils...?"

"Pens," Maggie said, her voice triumphant. "In this case, quill pens. *Lines of love*...I think..."

Zak met Maggie's gaze. "A love letter. That's what this means."

"Okay." Maggie looked out the window. "A love letter *locked in a prison of glass*."

"Seems to me a glass prison would be pretty easy to break out of," Zak said.

She frowned. "Yes, but this is a piece of paper—we're assuming—so someone put it somewhere."

"Inside something, maybe, where it couldn't get out."

"Or couldn't be gotten out of," Maggie countered.

"So," Zak said, and joined her by the window, "Where are places you can't get in to or out of easily?"

"Jail," Maggie said.

"A prison," Zak murmured. "What else

could be a prison?"

"A glass prison…" Maggie said. "Someone put it somewhere…"

"Like in a jar," Zak said.

"Or a bottle." Maggie stopped and stared at him. "That's it. A bottle. A glass bottle. The love letter is inside a bottle."

"Which makes perfect sense, given the time period and the people," Zak said. "The question is, where?"

"Well," Maggie said, "if the first part of the riddle was in *these* letters, then it stands to reason the other part might be in something else that Kidd wrote?"

"That'd be a logical place to start," Zak said, "and if we follow that line of reasoning, we should take a look at that fragmentary third letter."

"Your granddad still has it?" Maggie asked.

Zak nodded. "I left it with him at his cottage."

"Okay," Maggie said. "Let's go look at it."

Zak glanced at his watch. "Let's meet up there tomorrow. I need to check in with my team on their progress and put in some hours on the boat for the remainder of today."

"Right," Maggie said, "tomorrow it is."

THE NEXT MORNING, after Maggie took a shower, she headed to her suitcase on top of the bureau and pulled out a butter-yellow top. But where were her white capris? She glanced at the sea chest, which she'd placed beside her suitcase last night after they'd gotten back from Eddie's. Surely she hadn't put her capris underneath the chest by accident?

She reached out to pick it up and check, just in case. But age and mice had eaten away at the leather handles, and as she moved the chest, they gave way. The chest fell onto the floor with a thud and hit hard on one of the corners, which caused the lid to snap off at the hinges. Maggie looked down at it. Crap.

She crouched down and stared hard at the lining's red pinstripe pattern. She cocked her head. It seemed at odds with the heavy square-headed nails that held the half-rotted box together.

She shook her head. Eddie certainly had an eye for oddities. She touched the lining. The material felt rough, uneven. As if someone hadn't attached it correctly. She frowned as she brushed her fingers along the underside of the lid, near some burn marks. The lining wasn't flush against the top of the lid—as if it concealed a small hiding place.

Very slowly, she peeled away the faded lining. Her fingers encountered...ribbon? And a thick folded page. She slowly pulled the sheet of paper out and undid the bow. The ribbon fell away from her fingertips. She picked up the sheet. No name was written on the folded page. A shiver went through her. She flipped the folded page over and ran a finger across the faded red wax before she gently broke the seal and unfolded the paper.

Coastal waters of Spanish St. Augustine
1 June 1700   *Henry Davies*

Dearest Henry,

Oh, how my heart beats with gladness at receiving Word that your year-long trek West has successfully begun, as it means your travels come to a close in June next. And that you shall, within six weeks after your

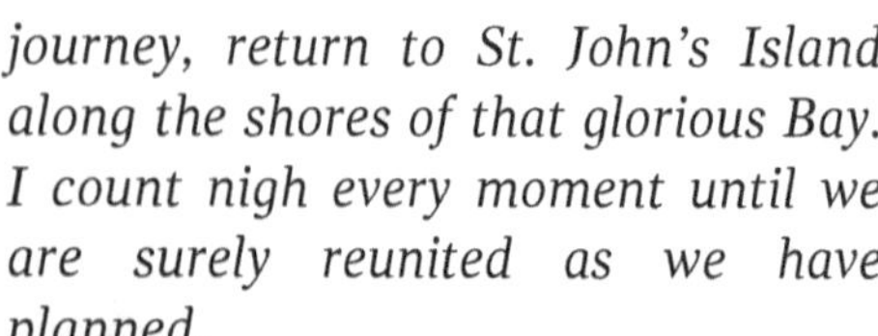

journey, return to St. John's Island along the shores of that glorious Bay. I count nigh every moment until we are surely reunited as we have planned.

You may recall what I had written you some months ago. Those who would have me burned as a witch may quiver in fear and small-mindedness; nonetheless, what I have foreseen has come to pass.

I tried to give Kidd aide, as he had so assisted me, yet I fear I was unsuccessful. He has been accused of piracy and travelled to New York in an effort to have the warrant rescinded last June. As he now has been jailed for nigh a year, I fear for his life.

Though, I must confess, I do not fear for my own, as I know how to wield a dagger though I am reluctant to use one on my own Quartermaster, James Fitzhugh.

Yet twice I have seen him skulking about during our journey northward from the jungles of the Amazon, exerting himself in trying to break open my quarters.

In search, no doubt, not only for the doubloons I intend for our wedded life, but also for the necklace I always wear. (Though few know of its Origins—except, mayhap, the wise woman who bequeathed it to me—and fewer still its Foretelling of true Love.)

But that look in his eye leaves me little doubt as to his other intentions, though he knows full well of your & my Understanding. Only the sharpness of my blade has thwarted his unwelcome advances upon my person & my purse.

I should never have agreed to take him aboard. He grows more belligerent daily, and I do wonder if his ill manners and disrespect affect the rest of the crew.

Beloved, I shan't worry you any longer. All shall be well. I shall see to it myself. Now my candle flame gutters, so I must bid you a Good night.

All my love,
Eleanor

She had to tell Zak about this. He'd love to add this new information to his research about the ship. Not only that, the initials *J.F.* that Eddie pointed out must mean that this chest had been owned by James Fitzhugh. He must have kept, and hidden, Eleanor's letter because of his jealousy.

And suddenly, another thought struck her. She could use excerpts from this letter in the story behind the new piece and in the packaging of the jewelry box.

Hmmm. She'd have to run it by Jia once she heard back from her. She could even make the presentation box look like an antique letter with a ribbon around it? Yes. That could definitely work. Maggie's mind churned with possibilities. She hadn't yet heard from Zak about when he wanted her to meet him at Dalvay. So she began to jot notes around the edges of the mood board she'd created for the pendant.

Fabric swatches, bits of shiny foil in delicate designs, glossy pictures of Spanish galleons, and a copy of the pencil sketch of Eleanor, were all pinned to it. She studied the woman's expression again and smiled. They had to find the pendant and find out the rest of her story.

But the ringing of the phone tore Maggie's attention away from her thoughts about Eleanor. She answered it on the first ring. "Maggie speaking."

"Hi Maggie, this is Jia."

Maggie's pulse pounded.

"We received your photo of the sketch."

Maggie pulled out the drawing for reference.

"Yes," a man's voice said. "I'm Mike, the head of the design team."

"Okay, great." Maggie said. She did her best to suppress the tremor of nervousness in her tone.

A pause.

"Well," Jia said, and then cleared her throat. "This is..."

"...certainly creative," Mike said.

"Yes, very," Jia added.

"But," Mike said, "we can't accept it."

"The thing is, it's not in line with the vision of your bracelet." Jia said.

"What else do you have for us?" Mike asked.

Crap. Maggie licked her dry lips and straightened her spine. "I just have the one

design at the moment."

"Mmm," Mike said. Maggie could almost hear his frown.

She stared at her mood board and felt hot tears at the edges of her eyes. No. She wasn't going to cry now. She blinked the tears back fiercely.

"Well, if that's all you have for us, that's not what Courtney Jewelers wants to pursue," Jia said.

Maggie's heart fell to her toes.

"So," Jia said, "we won't be using your design."

Maggie swallowed down the lump in her throat and gripped the phone. Her gaze travelled to the copy of Eleanor's picture on the mood board. She couldn't let Eleanor down now.

"Please know it's nothing personal," Jia said, her voice cheery.

"Just business," Mike added.

Maggie took a breath. "Of course." She forced lightness into her tone even as she crumpled the drawing up into a tiny wad and shoved it deep into her purse. "No problem at all."

"But your bracelet's doing so well, we're going to carry that. We'll be in touch about arranging the paperwork for you to come in and sign. Have a great day!" Jia said, just before she ended the call.

Maggie put the phone down with a shaking hand and bit her lip. No. She shook her head. She wasn't going to use their rejection of her design as an excuse to run away or give up. Her gaze strayed back to the mood board and Eleanor's picture. She was going to treat this as a reason to stay, to fight for what she believed in, and to win.

Yes. She lifted her chin. Eleanor probably would've approved of her plan.

Besides, she had to look on the bright side. At least Courtney Jewelers had decided to carry her bracelet. And she and Zak were making definite progress on discovering the deeper connection between Eleanor, the pendant and the ship. And if—no—*when* they found the pendant, it would help both of their careers. Even if Zak *was* too stubborn to admit it. Who knew? Maybe when they found the pendant, that would even change the jewelry company's mind about her new design.

THAT SAME MORNING, Zak, who wore his Memorial University T-shirt and a holey pair of jeans, grabbed the day's *Guardian* off the porch. He'd have to leaf through it later. When he had time. He glanced at his watch, as if just by looking at it, he could give himself more time to find the shipwreck and finish the book.

His cellphone buzzed with a text from Maggie. *Zak, guess what I just found—a letter in the sea chest that mentions Davies AND the pendant! I'll bring it with me when I see you today. By the way, when are we going to go up there? Oh, and apparently, J.F. on the chest stands for James Fitzhugh, the quartermaster on* Lady's Revenge.

Hmmm. This could be really useful.

Great work, Maggie! :) Thanks for letting me know. You can head on up if you want. I'll meet you there in about an hour. I want to check if there's any reference to that kind of thing in Davies' travel journal first. Zak hit send and then went into his temporary office.

Maybe he could find something about a letter in Davies' journal. He hefted the volume and started to leaf through it. But he paused when he got to the thicker-than-normal section. Could this section be concealing something important? Maybe even relating to the letter Maggie had mentioned? He ran his fingers lightly along the edge of the antique paper.

He examined the paper more closely. Then rooted around in a drawer until he found a pair of tweezers.

Very carefully, he peeled away the edges to reveal...a letter.

He looked down at the water-stained and warped sheet.

Port Royal, Jamaica
3 March 1699   *Henry Davies*

Dearest Henry,

Oh glorious day! My love, I have the happiest of news. Kidd surely made good on his promise of obtaining me a command—and a new and faster ship. Not only that, but I have also begun amassing a crew.

One of Kidd's former crewmen— you know of whom I speak—though I have duly made efforts to dissuade him, has come aboard the Lady's

Revenge as Quartermaster. For what reasons I cannot foretell. I fear they be not entirely pleasant nor good. (Though, with a ship such as mine, not employed in altogether legal activities, perhaps pleasant and good are too generous of words.)

I fear 'tis too late to undo what has been done.

The other man—Nicholas Mac-Donald—has joined my ranks as First Mate. 'Tis fortunate indeed, as he, also a former Kidd crewman, I trust entirely.

Oh, but how the lines and sails of this ship remind me of another deck on another sea, with your arms 'round my waist.

I cannot but smile at the memory of your face as you thought me to be a lady among a ship full of cutthroats when you came aboard in the Far East...

It feels an age since I last laid eyes upon your dear countenance. Though I must have faith that we shall again be united, once your western trek with the Hudson's Bay

Company has ended. I confess, I shall rest easy once you have safely rejoined that Mi'kmaq settlement on St. John's Island.

I wish you fare well for now, dearest. Though I fear to disclose too much in a missive such as this, I feel I must, nonetheless, unburden myself in your good confidence.

Love, do take care. I await your return to the shores of that Beloved Isle with much anticipation.

Always yours,
Eleanor

Hmm. A primary source would certainly be of interest to his readers. Maybe he could add this to his book.

Zak grinned. He had to tell Maggie. Now they both had letters to show each other. He glanced at his watch. Speaking of which, he had to head over to talk to Granddad.

MAGGIE GLANCED AT the clock on the dash, turned off her rental car and stepped out

into the parking lot at Dalvay. She'd gotten here pretty early. Might as well wait for Zak inside the main house. Then they could go to his granddad's together.

She strode into the hotel and looked around. A large sandstone fireplace was adjacent to her, in what was now the lobby but was originally the foyer of the house. Heavy wood panelling lined the space. A wide staircase spanned the opposite end of the room and led to the open second floor.

Some summer cottage. Maggie shook her head. She paused to adjust her car keys, which had started to work their way out of her pocket. Then she texted Zak. *When you get here, I'll be in the main house.* As Maggie wandered across the maroon floral runner, she noticed a couple at the check-in desk. They stood with their backs to her. She cocked her head as their conversation with the front desk clerk caught her ear.

"Where should we put it?" the woman asked the clerk. She waved a hand to indicate the small drop-front writing desk with delicately turned legs next to her.

"My manager told me we should put it in the side parlor over here since it's an original piece owned by Mr. Alexander MacDonald." The clerk came out from behind the counter. "Here, I'll help you guys move it. We want our guests to enjoy the history."

Maggie frowned and looked again at the woman. Was that...Ruby and Nathan? Maggie took a step closer to the pair. Last she'd heard from her friend, they'd still been in Ireland.

The man spoke again. "My mom knew the MacDonalds. And when I discovered that she'd intended to give the desk back after she found out who'd originally owned it, I wanted to donate it here where it belongs. Mom bought it at an auction in North Rustico. For years I thought the desk was Federal style but Ruby here—" he slid an arm around the woman's waist "—told me it's from an earlier period." He grinned at her and Maggie saw the warmth in his gaze.

"Right," Ruby said as she smiled back at Nathan. "It's actually an early Baroque drop-front writing desk. We've done some research on the piece and found out Alexander MacDonald's ancestor Nicholas MacDonald originally owned it. He'd

imported it from New York."

Maggie's eyes widened.

Nathan picked up one side of the desk and the clerk picked up the other side. They started to move it to the parlor.

"Ruby!" Maggie called out, before she could follow the two men.

Ruby turned at the sound of her name. "Maggie?" She laughed and they hugged. "What are you doing here?"

"I could ask you the same thing." Maggie smiled. "It's so good to see you."

"We just got back from Dublin yesterday." Ruby beamed.

"I'm so happy for you guys," Maggie said.

"And we're here now because Nathan wanted to drop off the desk before he starts work again in a few days," Ruby said.

Maggie nodded. "I'm on the island here doing some research for a new jewelry piece. I'd love to look at that desk, actually," Maggie said.

"Oh sure," Ruby said, "Come on."

The two women headed into the parlor as the clerk went back to the front desk.

After Maggie said hello to Nathan, she looked at the desk. "It's beautiful." The exterior of the drop-front writing surface was inlaid along the edges with an intricate marquetry pattern. "Can I...?" Maggie reached out a hand.

"Sure," Nathan said. He pulled out his phone and turned to Ruby as Maggie heard him say, "So the realtor thought these would be good options for us."

Out of the corner of her eye, Maggie saw them head to a couch on the other side of the room. Maggie lowered the writing surface. Inside, tiny compartments and drawers with mother-of-pearl knobs spanned the back of the space. She leaned forward to examine the brightly polished knobs. Oops. Her car keys slipped out of her front jeans pocket and landed on the floor on top of the air conditioning vent.

Maggie bent to retrieve them. But the vent caught the lightweight keychain so that it stuck in the grill, which was partially underneath the desk. As she crouched down, she accidently banged her knee against the front of the desk when she reached farther forward to grab the keys. She started to straighten up. But as she did, the moulding along the bottom of the desk caught her eye. It appeared to have come loose.

Crap.

Had she broken it when she banged her knee? She scooted closer and frowned. No. The moulding had fallen forward at a forty-five degree angle as if it had been hinged to do that. She tucked a strand of hair behind her ear and peered closer. Was that a...lever hidden behind the moulding? She reached out her hand.

Why would—

"Lose something, Maggie?" Zak's voice made the hairs on the back of her neck rise.

She swivelled her head and saw him enter the room. "Oh! Zak. I, uh," she stood up and darted a glance at Ruby and Nathan, who had looked up from their spot on the couch.

"Ruby, Nathan, this is Zak Stuart," Maggie said.

Zak nodded a hello to Ruby and Nathan, who got up from the couch and crossed the room in Maggie and Zak's direction. "Hi, how are ya, Zak?" Nathan said. The two men shook hands.

"Nice to meet you, Zak," Ruby said. He nodded back at her.

"I think I found some sort of lever...here," Maggie said to the three others. "Mind if I show Zak?"

Ruby nudged Nathan and a knowing look passed between them. "You two go ahead. We're gonna keep looking at real estate listings." They headed back to the couch.

A blush heated Maggie's cheeks. To cover for it, she whispered to Zak as she crouched down. "Do you know whose desk this is?"

Zak shook his head and crouched down beside her, so close that his shoulder brushed against hers. She couldn't bring herself to move away.

"Nicholas   MacDonald's."   Maggie reached up and brushed her fingers against the tiny lever. Yes. Cool metal. "I think there's a hidden compartment here."

Zak gave her a speculative look.

"Only one way to find out." She pressed her fingers against the lever. There was a faint ping but when she examined the front of the desk, nothing seemed to have changed.

Zak leaned first to the left and then the right. "Nothing on either side."

"Which means..." Maggie trailed off.

She shifted position at the same time Zak did.

"We need to look underneath," Zak finished.

She lay on her back beside Zak on the plush hand-woven carpet. "Look," Maggie whispered as she pointed at the underside of the desk, near the maker's mark.

"Some sort of panel's been triggered," Zak said. His fingertips brushed against her arm as he reached up to press the panel.

She sucked in a breath as the secret panel popped open to reveal a faded, torn and blackened sheet of paper. Zak's eyes slid to hers and a grin spread across his face. For a second, she was seventeen again. Her heart banged against her ribs. He was so near... If she moved just a fraction, she could close the space between them, taste his—No. She moved her hand toward the page instead and closed her fingers around it. But her eyes remained fastened on Zak's.

A sudden burst of staccato German near the entrance to the room made them both scramble out from under the desk and jump apart. Zak turned back to hastily close the hidden compartment. Maggie smoothed her hair as he adjusted his T-shirt. The loudly-chattering cluster of tourists walked right by the doorway. Maggie coughed. Zak cleared his throat.

"We found, um, a letter," Maggie held it up for Ruby and Nathan to see.

"Wow," Ruby said. She gestured to Nathan and they walked over.

"Yeah, it's—" Zak stopped mid-sentence. His warm fingers brushed Maggie's as she held the page and his eyes grew round as he pointed at the fragment Maggie held. "I think this might be the missing piece of Kidd's third letter that Granddad has."

"Take it," Nathan said. "If it'll help you find whatever you guys are looking for, then you can have it."

Ruby laughed. "You two must be solving some sort of island mystery. Well, have fun." She shared a look with Nathan. "We know what that's like, don't we?"

Nathan grinned at Ruby and interlaced his fingers with hers. "Sure do—we figured out what happened to the lost Great Seal of Prince Edward Island."

"But that's a long story," Ruby said. "Listen, it was great to see you, Maggie,

and meet you, Zak, but we should get going. Lots to do now that we're back from our honeymoon. And we should definitely catch up soon, Maggie."

"That'd be great, Ruby," Maggie said. Ruby and Nathan waved as they left. A few minutes later, Zak and Maggie stood on the small cottage porch.

Zak knocked on the doorframe. "Granddad?" he called.

"Come on in, kids," Ian called. "I'm just watching some TV."

Zak and Maggie went inside. "I think we found the rest of Kidd's third letter," Zak said to his grandfather.

"Did you now?" Ian flicked off the television set. "Let me just go get the fragments and we can take a look." He returned a few minutes later with the Ziploc baggie in hand and handed it to Zak.

Maggie held up the fragment they'd found and Zak compared it with his. "Yes. This is a definite fit."

—ubloons than what she is due, as I feel I owe her for her kind Assistance in attempting to warn me of my Ordeals with the Crown.

Thus, I ask that you deliver to her the Gold, as I cannot.

I remain, as always, your Loyal friend,

"So Kidd paid Eleanor for her help," Zak said. "That's what she meant in those letters, and that's why everyone thought the treasure was Kidd's. But it wasn't—not really. He'd given some of his gold to Eleanor."

"That makes sense," Maggie said. Her brows rose. "And look." She pointed to the page. "Those same ink blots and quill drag marks."

"More of the cipher," Zak said.

"You were right, Zak." Maggie rummaged around in her purse and got out a pen and paper and began to jot down the ciphered text alongside the key she'd drawn earlier. She pursed her lips. "This is the second half of the riddle, then."

—a N.W. circle of water
Meets the Gulf's embrace.

Zak shook his head. "Some sort of location?"

"Let's go over the whole thing, then." Maggie said. "*Lines of love/locked in a prison of glass/where a N.W. circle of water/meets the Gulf's embrace.*" She tapped her finger against her chin.

"*N.W.* must mean northwest," Zak said.

"And it's near the gulf. Probably the Gulf of the St. Lawrence, given the history of everything else." Maggie added.

"That's a safe bet." Zak nodded.

"So a circle of water. Like a pond."

"Or a lake. Near the gulf."

"Just a second," Ian interjected. "I have a sea chart around here somewhere..." He rooted around on a nearby shelf and then handed Zak a creased and faded chart. Zak unfolded it and began to search the area where the Gulf of St. Lawrence met Prince Edward Island's north shore.

"Oh," Zak said.

"What?" Maggie asked.

"There's lots of small inlets and seaside lakes along the north shore," Zak said. "But," he pointed a finger at the map, "here's one on Dalvay property."

"I bet that's it." She peered at the map. "Especially since it's practically a literal circle of water. At least we don't have to go far."

"Mmm. Might be worth taking a look." Zak said. He raked a hand through his hair. "I need to head back to the boat for the rest of the day. But how about we meet back here at that little lake first thing tomorrow?"

THE NEXT MORNING, Maggie took a sip of her Tim Horton's latte and looked out at the view.

The sand shifted underfoot even as the crash of waves reached Maggie's ears, along with the deep timbre of Zak's voice. "This spot at Dalvay is beautiful, isn't it?"

"It is," Maggie said as she turned and smiled at him. "Morning."

Zak glanced at her sharply. "Hard to believe in maybe seventy years, this probably won't be here. Coastline's disappearing at the rate of about two centimeters per year, thanks to global warming." He crossed his arms.

"Zak," Maggie said as she shifted her weight, "what's going on?"

"This." He held up a copy of the Charlottetown paper.

"Don't tell me," Zak's tone was cold, "that this is what I think it is." He pointed to a headline at the bottom of the front page.

*Story of Stuart Family Treasure
Breaks Sales Records*

Reprinted from
The New York Sun

Charlottetown, Canada—AP *Just a few short months ago, Prince Edward Islander Maggie Kilhoughery was an unknown jewelry designer looking for a way to fame and fortune in New York City.*

And then she struck gold. Literally.

Kilhoughery broke retail sales records when she used the previously-unknown family history of nautical archaeologist Dr. Zachary Stuart—a descendant of treasure hunter Samuel Stuart—to launch the first piece in her debut jewelry line Treasured Oceans of Love *in a social media campaign that went viral.*

"We've hit half a million followers and nearly double that in sales. It's great," Kilhoughery said.

Captain William Kidd, whose treasure has long been associated with Prince Edward Island, was the reason for the jewelry line's creation.

According to Kilhoughery's social media campaign, Kidd had given gold to Stuart's ancestors, which Charles Lewis Tiffany then used to create a bracelet. This antique bracelet became the inspiration for Kilhoughery's first piece in her own line.

Currently, Kilhoughery is working with Stuart to uncover more of Kidd's treasure as inspiration for her next piece. They hope to uncover a whole treasure ship. A search is under way at Bay Fortune.

Dr. Trevor Woods, head of the nautical archaeology department at Memorial University, confirmed that grant money had been given for a shipwreck survey project in the Bay Fortune area.

The Stuart family was unable to be reached for comment.

Maggie bit her lip before she forced herself to look into his eyes. "It is." She swallowed.

Zak didn't reply.

Maggie tapped her foot. "Zak, you're the one who gave me the antique bracelet in the first place."

Still, Zak said nothing.

Maggie put her hands on her hips. "In that social media campaign, I was careful not to mention you by name. I didn't even tell anyone here," Maggie said, "so I don't know how the *Sun* got all this information." She gestured to the page.

"You expect me to believe that? It's P.E.I." His eyes flashed. "People talk! If it's not a neighbor minding your business, it's a cousin of your sister-in-law. Or your neighbor *is* a cousin of your sister-in-law. They all want to mind everyone's business like it's their own." Zak's tone turned bitter. "But that's not even the worst part. You know what is? This article," he jabbed a finger at the headline, "is implying I'm a treasure hunter. Do you know what this'll look like to my colleagues? What it could do to my career?"

He didn't let Maggie respond.

"Worse, there'll be hoards of treasure seekers here—" His voice became brittle. Angry. "—jeopardizing the integrity of the archaeological site. And there's nothing we can do about it."

"Zak, it's not like I did it on purpose."

She crossed her arms.

"Then why is CBC covering it? And," he added, "it's on *The New York Times'* website."

"What?" Maggie's eyes widened.

Zak shook his head. "You only thought about yourself, didn't you?"

Her breath hitched. She opened her mouth then closed it.

Zak continued. "You basically steal your *inspiration* from my family's history, come here, take advantage of what my research can give you—" he clenched his hands into fists "—and then leave."

He averted his eyes just as Maggie saw the beginnings of real hurt, vulnerability, in their hazel depths. "I was stupid enough to trust you about our research, our working together."

She couldn't say anything to make him believe her, could she? Her bottom lip trembled but she forced herself to remain calm. Unfeeling. But that was...impossible.

Yet she spoke anyway. "Can't you just trust me on this?" She forced herself to tamp down her growing irritation at Zak. "I came up here—" she dragged the words out with near super-human effort "—to find out more about Eleanor Webster because I thought it would help me with my next piece. I wasn't...trying to wreck your reputation or steal from you. And I didn't do that with the antique bracelet, either."

"No?" He laughed—an empty sound. "Certainly didn't look like that from where I stood. *Am* standing." His gaze bored into hers.

"Just because you gave me the bracelet for my birthday that one year doesn't mean you can tell me what to do with it. Especially not now." She lifted her chin.

Zak's gaze hardened. "You never gave it back. You should have when we broke up. It was a valuable piece of my family's history that you kept for yourself."

"Oh, so this is all my fault?" she said, as her temper rose. "Come on, Zak. I don't want to hear it. Be reasonable. It was a *gift* you gave me. I shouldn't have to give it back to you just because we broke up. And for your information," she shot back, as hurt threaded through her, "I *did* think about giving it back to you. But I—" she blinked back sudden hot tears "—just couldn't," she whispered. She swallowed down a lump in her throat and her anger rose to the surface again. "All you care about—ever cared about—is your stupid scientific projects and lectures. You never wanted to help me with my jewelry design research, did you? You just used that as an excuse to find out whatever you could about *Lady's Revenge*." Maggie pressed her lips together. "You're not being fair to me. And I think you know a thing or two about *that*. You asked me to stay on the island here when you knew—you *knew*—" she jabbed a finger at his chest "—that my dream was to go to design school in New York City. It was totally unfair of you to ask me to stay. You expected me to give up my dreams for you."

God. Her fingers flexed. Didn't he care how she felt? Didn't he care... at all? And for one, two...three unreasonable moments, she hated him for it.

"You don't know the first thing about fairness, Maggie. You betrayed my trust in you when you broke my heart in high school then refused my proposal—" Zak broke off and clenched his hands. "I thought everything was great. I thought you'd *want* to say yes. I thought you actually loved me. But the only thing you loved was your damn career." He narrowed his eyes at her. "And I was idiot enough to think you'd changed." He shook his head. "Obviously, three years hasn't changed you at all." Zak glared at her.

Maggie glared back. "Just because we're working together, just because we happen to be solving these riddles, that means you have some license to—"

"—Working together? You think we're still working together? After all this?" He folded his arms across his chest. "We're through. And now, it's for good."

Chapter Seven

ZAK FANNED THE sea floor with his gloved hand. It was the best way to search for anything that might be hiding just under the surface.

He grimaced. Why had he fought with Maggie? Things had been going so well and if he was completely honest, he'd begun to hope—No. There was no point in thinking about what might have been. That's what had gotten him into trouble before.

But he could see her eyes alight, her windblown chocolate-brown hair, and her laughter as they'd eaten dinner at Sheltered Harbour Cafe. He swallowed, tried to push the image aside.

But as soon as he did, another, older memory popped up. This time, he could hear Maggie's voice in his head as she'd said, "Do you think we really have a good chance of finding anything?" Hope had mixed with skepticism in her expression. He'd had to do a fair bit of cajoling, and—his lips quirked upward—had to give more than a kiss or two, to persuade her that the romance of the adventure was almost as exciting as *actually* finding something. He could almost smell her sunscreen again. Taste the salt on her lips as the sea spray had rocked his sail boat and the sun had sparkled on the July waters. Cherry lip gloss. That's what she had always used, wasn't it?

He shook himself. What was he doing?

He rubbed the back of his neck. He'd always been a sentimentalist. But something about this dive, he supposed, had it all rushing back to him. Back when it seemed so easy. So simple. As if gold and jewels lay at the bottom of every craggy ocean outcropping. He opened his eyes and looked down at the sea floor.

No treasure here.

But he had spotted a few boats in the previously empty area where the research vessel had dropped anchor. He scowled. Treasure hunters. Because of that damn *Guardian* reprint. He pushed aside those thoughts and tried to concentrate again. If he moped about Maggie, it wasn't going to help him find the wreck. In fact, it might even make things worse. He could miss the tiniest detail.

Clouds of sand billowed around him as he brushed at the sea floor. He was about to move to another spot when a barnacle-encrusted object caught his eye.

He picked it up.

Small and light with a familiar shape. A dagger? From what was left of the curved blade, he'd guess Spanish. He tucked it into his dive bag and kept up his search. The dagger might mean an actual debris trail this time. And a debris trail—depending on the age of the artifacts—could very possibly lead to the wreck. He hoped.

He gave a mental sigh. They only had two weeks left on the deadline. Besides, if they didn't find a solid lead soon, the morale of everyone involved in the whole project would plummet even further. He wasn't sure he could take that. Work was the only thing left to hold onto. And he wasn't going to allow anything to drown out his love for his career.

He returned his attention to the seabed and moved a few centimeters from where he'd found the dagger. Only sand. Just then he felt a tap on his shoulder. His dive partner held up what looked like, as far as Zak could guess, a spoon. He nodded to the other person and they ascended to examine their findings.

Zak stripped out of his dry suit and shrugged into comfortable clothes.

"Set these in solution and then we can take a look at them," Zak said to his assistant, and headed into the makeshift lab set up next door to their computers.

But after the solution had cleaned away the centuries of accumulation, Zak's heart fell. The spoon wasn't from the right time period. And, while the dagger was from the 17th century, that didn't prove anything concrete. His lips compressed. He'd have to call a meeting.

Ten minutes later, everyone sat around the small kitchen table in the galley. "You all know how long we've been at this now, and we haven't found anything conclusive or useful. We're going to have to change tactics. Look in a few new places that will help us narrow the search area down even further. That means we'll need to take some time away from the water. Talk to locals. Go through the reports and logs we've already gathered to see if we can find new leads to pinpoint a more specific area. Because this smattering of objects we've found so far—" he held up the spoon, the dagger and the musket ball "—aren't enough to warrant funding for a full-scale excavation. We *need* to find a shipwreck."

AFTER AN AIMLESS day of wandering through the historic streets of downtown Charlottetown, Maggie headed back to her hotel room that night and tried to smooth down her windblown ponytail. Where was her hairbrush? She glanced at her reflection in the mirror above the bureau where the sea chest and suitcase sat. She gave herself a watery smile. "What am I going to do?" she murmured. There had to be a solution. She sighed and slid out of her shoes.

A sense of sadness welled within her. What if Zak had been right all along? That she'd been the bad guy in the whole thing? She winced. No. She couldn't think like that.

Maybe this turn of events was actually a good thing? Maybe this was exactly what she needed? Maybe she was exactly where she needed to be, too?

She glanced at the mood board she'd created. All at once, realization came crashing down.

She'd relied too much on waiting for inspiration to strike. She'd called it legitimate research, when really it had been a smoke screen for her fears. Her fears that, without having a framework, something to guide her—in this case, Eleanor's personal history—she wouldn't be able to really do her art justice or be a real artist.

She tried to shove the feeling aside, so she flipped on the TV. But a sudden wave of deeper emotion made her pause. She pulled out the crumpled up sketch paper with her design from the bottom of her purse.

She caught her breath. Deep sorrow filled her as a long-ago memory surfaced: the feel of Zak's hands, warm against her skin, as they had watched the moon rise over the Northumberland Strait.

She should have done more, been

more, tried more, for him—with him. Three years ago. And today... She stared at the sketch. Zak was right. She'd been lying to herself. She'd been clinging to the hope that inspiration would save her. That inspiration—a muse—would give her the design she'd been hoping for. She'd been using the story of Eleanor and all that research as an excuse to stay blocked. An excuse to not dig deeper. She'd been afraid. Afraid to fail. Afraid she wouldn't be able to do it. Couldn't do it. Which is what Zak had meant.

She began to doodle along the edge of the crumpled page. She smoothed a hand over her messy ponytail even as she continued to absently draw on the paper. Anger and frustration welled up within her; the culmination of the last few weeks and months of work, and more work; and stress after stress. She tugged on the end of her ponytail and then pulled it free of the hair elastic.

Maggie needed some time off. Some time to relax, recover. She was supposed to be the founder of this company. But wasn't that what owning a company was all about? Working harder and longer than anyone else?

She shook her head, looked out the plate glass window and then down at her page again. Suddenly, she drew in a sharp breath. *That's* what had been lacking before. Why Courtney Jewelers had rejected this. Because this drawing...was incomplete.

ZAK SHOVED HIS hands deep into his jeans pockets as he walked over to his truck at the end of the day. He'd decided to take the dagger with him to study more closely at the house. Maybe it would yield some answers. This evening there had to be at least twice the number of vehicles along the dock here than there had been this morning.

A knot tied itself in his stomach. What if the treasure hunters found something conclusive before he did? Worse, what if they totally destroyed the archaeological integrity of the area? Not only that, he couldn't shake the feeling of disappointment about the search. And, if he was totally honest, about Maggie. His truck bounced down the dirt road toward the old

Victorian house. Damn it. She'd walked away. She couldn't just leave him. Except she had. Again.

No. That wasn't true. He'd pushed her away. He sighed and shook his head. Suddenly, he felt exhausted. It looked like Maggie was determined to be his enemy. Not that he'd done nothing. He'd participated in his fair share of less-than-stellar behaviors, after all.

Zak pulled to a stop in the driveway and headed inside with the dagger just as a full red-orange moon began to rise over his rooftop.

He went into the kitchen and made himself a cup of camomile tea then headed for the living room, where he put the dagger on the coffee table by Davies' journal. He stroked a finger along the hilt. A thrill ran through him. Almost as if he could reach out and touch the past. Whose was it? Where had it come from? Could it have belonged to someone on *Lady's Revenge*? Perhaps... or perhaps not.

He yawned and glanced out at the moon again. Its orangish light pooled across the floor. Something about the color reminded him of the dagger. He put the small knife down, scrubbed a hand across his face and sighed. He needed to get some sleep. He could look at his find more closely in the daylight.

After he'd showered, he pulled on his plaid flannel pajama bottoms and got in between the cool clean sheets. He yawned again and drifted off to sleep almost as soon as his head hit the pillow...

The wind whipped the rigging and made the main mast creak and groan as the dark clouds whirled and parted to reveal yellow-green light and flashes of lightning just past Zak's vision.

He frowned. Where was he? And why did it seem so vivid? He looked around. All was in darkness except for the bruised patch of sky above him, with the stars all wheeling around, it seemed, at top speed.

He looked around again. No one was here. What sort of dream was this? All he could see was highly polished decking surrounded by a burnished oak ship's rail. Coils of fat, tar-soaked rope were neatly piled on the deck beside leather buckets. And high above him, the rigging creaked and groaned around the reefed sails.

No crew. And no captain.

He walked up near-vertical steps. Headed toward the ship's wheel.

He felt his mind spin and a wave of dizziness wash over him. He managed to shake it off as he gripped the brass handrails more firmly then hauled himself onto the small raised platform with the ship's wheel and large ship's compass. Next to them was a map pinned to the back of a bench that ran along the side of the railing.

Zak reached a hand out to touch the faded, age-spotted map—in the shape of Prince Edward Island, he realized.

"I wouldn't do that if I were you."

At the sound of a low, feminine voice that sounded like bluebirds and brooks in spring, Zak whirled around.

His eyes met those of a tall woman with deep-set green eyes fringed with heavy dark lashes. Her long black hair was braided into a neat plait that circled her head like a crown. Her milk-white skin showed a long, jagged scar that ran in a delicate line from the top of her left cheekbone to just under her chin.

Zak blinked. Cocked his head.

She had a necklace around her throat. Silver and gold filigree rings studded with rubies, emeralds and sapphires sparkled on

her long fingers.

Fingers that gripped a jewel-hilted curved dagger. She wore a demure, polite smile; one that would, no doubt, not have been out of place in ballrooms and parlors, but one that now sent a shiver of apprehension down Zak's back. "Why not?" he managed at last, as he tore his gaze away from her sea-green one.

"Because 'tis wrong."

"Wrong? What do you mean?" He shook his head. Dreams had their own sort of logic.

The woman's lips curved upward even more. "Oh," she said, jewels winking in the moonlight, "'tis no dream."

Zak took a step toward her and his heart quickened. "Then tell me what to do. Tell me where the treasure is. Where the shipwreck is"

"Ah, you're a quick one. The others weren't, so much. They had grown fat and lazy, their minds dulled by greed. And..." She reached out and tapped the butt of the dagger against his chest. "Their hearts were not so recently bruised by heartache. I've waited a long time for one such as yourself."

He did a double take as she lowered the dagger. It looked exactly like the one he'd found. "So you're...Eleanor, I imagine."

"I am nothing you imagine, Zachary Stuart. No," she waved a hand, "this place is its own sort of reality. After all, it is the realm in which I reside. Me and my doomed crew aboard the Lady's Revenge.*" She waved a hand again, and Zak saw once more exactly what he'd seen that night at Argyle Shore. He blinked, and the images faded, leaving only the two of them on the tall ship sailing its way amid the stars.*

"My crew only appears when the moon is right," she said as she slid a finger along the curved sharpness of the dagger. "When I relive the pain of heartbreak once again. 'Tis a certain purity in the pain." She reached up and touched the necklace, and that's when Zak noticed that the large central pendant was missing. He blinked. How did he—The legend. In The Prince Edward Island Magazine. *His breath quickened. This was* real. *And he was* here.

The woman nodded. "Yes. It is as you recall. Every word of that so-called legend is not so-called fiction. 'Tis real." The pirate queen looked at Zak. Her eyes were more brilliant than the most brilliant emeralds. "That's why, Zachary, you have to help me. Help me, free my crew, and the treasure will be yours. The treasure of your heart."

"You're telling me that if I help you, I won't get your treasure but I will get Maggie back?"

"She has to come back to you of her own volition. I'm no witch." The pirate queen laughed. "But sometimes, I can see the future." She shook her head. "But I didn't that day. Oh, I could've listened. If I had, I wouldn't linger in this...realm. But I thought I knew. And because of that, you and I have, shall we say, a commonality."

Zak shoved his hands in his pockets. "And if I don't help you?"

The clouds scuttled across the moon, and a chill wind swept through Zak's hair, which caused goose bumps to appear on his skin.

"I think you know the answer to that already." She placed a fingertip on his chest where his heart beat rapidly.

Zak nodded. "Let me guess. There's some sort of curse if I don't help you, that will—"

"Ah, you've been reading many a tall tale, I see," Eleanor said as she fingered the necklace at her throat. "No," she said quietly, "no curse. Just everlasting regret for what could have been, but now never shall be." She shrugged and turned her back to Zak. "I cannot pass on to my Beloved, unless the *pendant is reclaimed by those of pure heart. Though 'twas my own choice, not by any curse. You see, I linger here because I desire justice to be served. For the man who stole my life, my pendant—and kept me from rejoining my love on that cold July night." She studied the rapid track of the clouds across the sky. "Oh, they tried to burn me for a witch. But I escaped and became a queen. Ah, it seems but a fortnight ago... I was born into Puritan faith, but when I foolishly took my sister into my confidence in an instance of second sight, she believed I'd turned to darkest witchcraft. 'Twas a sham of a trial. I slipped my bonds and escaped—with a souvenir." She gestured to her face. "So I took to the seas. I'd sailed to India where I met a wise woman. She gifted me the pendant. She saw what others did not, could not; that I had a pure heart. She told me that when I met my true love, my heart would glow just as the pendant would. By such manner, I would know that I could trust myself; could open my heart to the echoes of love within. As soon as she gifted me the pendant, things began to happen. I met Henry. Then, thanks to Kidd, I procured a new ship of my own, after the one I'd stolen from my father was commandeered by the British Navy." She watched the stars wheel overhead. Stopped speaking so long Zak thought she'd forgotten his presence. "Remember," she said at last, "if you do decide to help me, your heart must be pure."*

Zak shifted his weight and shoved his hands deeper into his pockets. "Pure?"

"Purely open to love. Your true love. As 'tis now."

Zak took a breath and opened his mouth to speak, but all at once, his surroundings melted into blackness.

MAGGIE BEGAN TO trace the outline of a single teardrop on the crumpled page she'd dug from her purse. She gulped back another wave of sadness as the sorrow turned into something far deeper, more all-encompassing: regret, pain, remorse.

Her heart felt like a leaden balloon but her fingers continued to sketch. More teardrops blossomed on the page like small pearlescent reminders of—no, not reminders of, but in honor of—her time with, and her feelings for, Zak and their relationship.

And around the cluster of teardrops—

tiny seed pearls—she added delicate silver filigree in gentle swooping curlicues. With deft pencil strokes, she added more to the design. She felt her heart lighten, and a bubble of peace and joy rise within her. She almost held her breath as she let her pencil draw more and more. Tiny diamonds, caught between the delicate wisps of silver, shed rainbows of light across the entire design.

She paused. Took a breath.

But as she did so, the smell of burning wood filled her senses. Her pulse sped up, and she looked around. But nothing was on fire. Of course not. As she glanced around the room, she thought she caught a glimpse of emerald-green eyes reflected in the window. She put a hand to her throat. All at once, she could hear the newscaster's voice very clearly. She jumped. She'd forgotten the TV was on.

"...visitor numbers have increased noticeably, thanks to word of a supposed treasure buried on the island. Despite impending storms, hundreds of people have come to tiny Bay Fortune to seek its untold riches. CBC's Jaime MacNeil has more..."

Her fingers tightened on the remote as she grabbed it and turned off the TV. She fished around in her purse. Her hairbrush had to be in here somewhere.

Hundreds of people? Zak would be horrified. If he even bothered to care at all.

She slowly pulled out the brush. But as she did, a page also fell from her purse to the floor in a sudden, inexplicable breeze. A silvery sound of...wind chimes? Or was that laughter? reached her. She frowned. There weren't any wind chimes nearby...

She shrugged. Lifted the brush to her hair.

She had more important things to do than worry about how Zak felt. Or how she'd screwed everything up.

The page fluttered for a moment as it settled onto the floor while she started to move the brush through her hair. But it was too late to fix things. She couldn't just head back over there. She shook her head. That would do no good. Or would it? That was a lot of visitors... She bit her lip then sighed. What was done was done. She pulled her hair back into a tidy ponytail. Wasn't it?

She secured her hair with the elastic and then picked up the piece of paper to toss it in too, when she paused. What? She slowly turned the page over. Studied the burned edges. She couldn't throw this out. How had it gotten here, anyway? She frowned.

She slowly re-read the fragment of Kidd's letter and thought about the lines of the riddle.

The newscaster's words echoed through her mind again. She couldn't let some strangers get to the treasure or Eleanor's pendant. Or ruin Zak's shipwreck search.

She changed into her nightgown and got ready for bed.

She couldn't give up on her jewelry design, either. Least of all, on the pendant she hoped to create—now that she'd finally drawn something worthwhile. She looked down at the fine pencil strokes again. Tilted her head. Hmmm. It would look stunning if she made all those facets into diamonds...wouldn't it? Though she'd never done anything quite as showy as all that, before.

She tapped her finger against her chin. Perhaps this was yet another reason to hunt up Zak and talk to him face to face. She couldn't just stand by and do nothing. Yes. She had to fix things.

Chapter Eight

IN BETWEEN SIPS of strong hot Earl Gray tea, Zak blinked and stretched. Only 6:05 a.m. He shook his head. Normally he didn't get up nearly this early. A restlessness had seized him and he couldn't sleep.

He picked up the dagger and retrieved Eleanor's love letter but his thoughts turned to Maggie. She still needed that pendant of Eleanor's. He winced. He might've overreacted just a tad about that article. Where was Eleanor's pendant? He shook his head. And *where* was the ship? Did the love letter in a bottle have answers to both? He stood up and started to pace. Huh. He must've had some strange dreams last night. But try as he might, he couldn't remember a single one. Just a sense of seasickness and urgency. The black tea had begun to do its work, because, as he drained his second cup, the unsettled, rather nebulous feeling in his gut began to fade. Until he flicked on the morning news.

MAGGIE AWOKE IN the big queen-sized bed with a start. The blackout curtains only partially obscured the morning light that pooled onto the floor and she realized she still clutched the charred piece of Kidd's letter in her hand. The riddle ran through her mind again and filled her with a vague sense of restlessness.

Her eyes were drawn to the edge of dawn around the window frame, and she jumped up out of bed. The thin jersey knit of her pale pink nightgown brushed against her thighs as she padded barefoot to the window.

She hesitated only a moment before she drew the thick outer curtain aside in one firm movement. The swish of the drapes sounded loud in the quiet and darkness. It looked like the storm had held off so far. A yawn overcame her as a more insistent surge of restlessness washed through her. She tried to push it aside.

As Maggie moved aside the sheer inner

curtain, the jewelry sketch caught her eye. She didn't have to change the minds of the people at Courtney Jewelers, after all, did she? No. She didn't. Now that things with them had fallen apart, she had a certain sort of freedom. A freedom to create whatever she liked. Go in whatever direction she wanted, design whatever she wanted.

Maggie didn't have to be restricted by deadlines or expectations. Though she did want to make something beautiful for her customers to enjoy. And that, she realized, was what she loved the most. Designing. Creating. Not all the business-y stuff. She could leave that to other people. She could be a jewelry supplier to retailers. She didn't have to have her own store, her own staff.

Maybe, just maybe, she could even do all the designing and creating from her laptop? She wouldn't have to have a real office. She could go anywhere she wanted, then, with anyone...

She gazed out the window. But it was Zak's face that flitted through her mind. The way he'd stood there, his hazel eyes filled with such anger and betrayal during their recent argument. She bit her lip and began to pace. She'd messed everything up between them. Again.

She glanced over at the digital clock on the nightstand. 6:33 a.m.

The only way to fix this was to help him find the shipwreck and prove to him that she wasn't trying to ruin his career. On impulse, she picked up her cell phone and hit Zak's number but ended the call on the second ring and put the phone down. She had to go to Dalvay by herself. She had to find that love letter in a bottle for him and give it to him because it could be vital to helping him find the shipwreck.

She turned away from the window, grabbed her clothes and ducked into the bathroom, where she pulled on a pair of jeans and a long-sleeve green T-shirt. Then she got her purse, picked up the keys to her rental car and left the room.

"ISLANDERS BETTER KEEP a weather eye to the horizon today. It looks like the monster storms, which have been wreaking havoc all along the eastern seaboard, have decided to

pay Canada a visit. An extreme wind warning has been issued for the island today. The hurricane is predicted to hit the island late tomorrow. A rare occurrence, but not outside the realm of possibility. Still, we'd better all batten down the hatches, so to speak."

Zak turned off the TV and ate the last of his President's Choice chocolate chip granola cereal. He poured the rest of his tea down the sink. And with it, the last of his good mood. Damn it.

He didn't have time to waste. He'd have to check in with his team. Might also have to fit in a dive today, too. A storm could stir up the sand and silt on the sea floor and they could lose what ground they'd gained.

Well, not if he could help it.

He crossed the room and grabbed his cell phone off the hall table. He sent a quick text to everyone. *Now that we've had some time to talk with locals and comb over our previous research, let's use the sonar to scan that new area closer in to the bay.*

His fingers tightened around the device as he turned it off silent mode and glanced down at it to see he'd missed a call earlier in the morning—from Maggie.

Did that mean she'd called to apologize? His heart leapt to his throat. He should be the one to call her back and apologize for fighting with her. Then offer to help her out somehow. Yes. That's what he needed to do. He punched in her number. It rang and rang. And rang. No answer.

Well, he'd just have to find out for himself if she'd gone where he guessed she had. Then he'd go straight back to Bay Fortune and his team.

He hopped in his pickup truck and headed for Dalvay.

THE DAWN SEEMED to follow Maggie's winding route to Dalvay as the riddle from Kidd's letters ran through her mind. If she could just find the love letter in the bottle...

She pulled into the lot and then headed for the small circular lake at the northwest corner of the Dalvay estate property.

The only sound in the silence was the call of gulls. She took a deep breath of cool, clean salt air. She had roots here. No, that wasn't true, exactly. She didn't have deep roots to this place; she had deep roots to Zak.

She never should have lied to him that evening at the lighthouse. All along, he'd been what she'd needed, and wanted.

She never should have gone looking for greener pastures. Never should've turned her back on him. She squeezed her eyes shut, rubbed her fingers underneath her eyes.

She took a step forward and took another deep breath.

But what if he didn't see it that way?

The wind whipped Maggie's hair back from her forehead.

Perhaps everything hadn't been lost? Perhaps this had been the only way...Things had to go off course so that she could see she'd been on the right track all along. The right track back to her heart and soul. The right track back to Zak.

She took another step. And the way forward right now was to uncover the letter, to prove to Zak that he could trust her, that she hadn't betrayed him after all, and that they were in fact on the same team. If she had enough time before the storm hit. Maggie shivered and rubbed her arms as the wind gusted. The tang of salt air stung her nose. The wind blew harder and stirred a frisson of apprehension in Maggie's stomach.

"Maggie!"

SHE TURNED AROUND. Zak stood a few feet behind her. She felt as if she'd been punched in the stomach. She folded her arms across her chest and blinked back sudden tears. "What are you doing here?"

"Looking for the next clue." Zak came to stand beside her. "And you."

Chapter Nine

"SO," MAGGIE SAID, "this is northwest."

Zak glanced at her. Strands of hair framed her face, and determination glinted in her eyes. She never looked more beautiful than when she had a gleam like that in her eyes. He gave an inward smile. She never had been one to give up, either.

He looked out at the wind-whipped surface of the small lake in the gray early morning light. He should apologize to her. Now was the perfect opportunity. But as his eyes flicked back to her face, all he saw was her expression as they'd argued. His mind went back to his resolution in the kitchen earlier that morning. How could a simple *I'm sorry* and some sort of fumbled explanation make up for years of hurt between them? He swallowed. It couldn't. Not really. He had to *show* her he'd changed. And the only way to do that was to help her find that pendant she needed. Work could wait for a little while.

Zak studied the horizon. It could be a pretty big storm. They had to get going. He took a step, and his foot scrabbled against something hard. He looked down, about to nudge whatever it was out of his way, but then he stopped.

"What is it?" Maggie came to stand by him. A hint of her perfume drifted to him. He reached down and picked up the bottle and turned it over in his hands. A faded label read 7Up.

Maggie threw her hands up into the air. "Well, I'm sure that wasn't around 300 years ago."

They continued to scan the sand. "This is pretty impossible. There's no way anything's left here now—" Zak almost tripped over a large gnarled pine tree root. The wind-ravaged tree was so bent and twisted that its age was impossible to tell. At the end of one of the tree roots, he noticed a large oddly shaped stone pitted with age and nearly filled with lichen. The roots seemed to intertwine themselves around the stone.

He crouched down and brushed his

fingertips against the rock. "Hmmm. These look like chisel marks on the surface here." Zak felt Maggie's warmth as she crouched beside him.

"I don't want to jump to any conclusions too quickly." He squinted. "But it looks like they form some sort of...symbol. A crown—with an X underneath."

"You're right," she said. As she reached out and traced the marks, her fingers brushed his and he had a sudden urge to interlace his fingers with hers.

They searched the sand around the rock. A deep shade of green caught Zak's eye. Not a root covered in green lichen but...something cylindrical.

He reached a hand out and felt it. It was, indeed, fuzzy with lichen and moss. And caked with sand. The daylight glinted and Zak picked up the object. It was heavy. A bottle. He turned it over in his hands.

A very old one.

He rubbed his thumb across it, which cleared away a layer of lichen and moss from the sides. Glass. Thick wavy green glass. But what a beautiful shade of green. Like the depths of the ocean mixed with sea foam. He held the bottle up to the daylight, and rubbed more of the moss and lichen away. As more of the glass was revealed, the light streamed more easily through the ancient bottle. His heart sped up. He tilted his head.

There was something inside.

The wind gusted. Zak flipped the bottle end for end so he could look directly down at the bottle's neck. Plugged with cork or wax? He couldn't quite tell, as it was completely blackened.

"Is this it?" Maggie said, a little breathless.

He met her gaze and grinned; he felt his anticipation mirror hers. "Only one way to find out." He reached for the Leatherman multi-tool he always kept in his back pocket but then he stopped. "We can't just open it here. We should take it over to the boat's lab, where we have more of a controlled environment."

"You should probably check in with your team, too, about the shipwreck?" Maggie said.

Zak nodded. But this was also important. He cradled the bottle as they picked their way back across the lawn and then over to their cars. "Come on, get in with me." He held open the Dodge's passenger door for her. "We can pick up your car later."

Maggie nodded and got in the passenger seat of his pickup. As Zak shut the door, he couldn't help but remember all the times he'd held the door for her before. He got in the driver's side and placed the bottle carefully beside him on the seat. He shut his door just as the wind gusted again.

He glanced out at the horizon and his stomach knotted. White cirrus clouds like that showed up before a storm. His pulse pounded. The weather reports looked like they were right. The storm would come soon. Too soon.

Only a matter of about thirty-six hours or so before it would reach here, too.

Forty minutes later, he pulled in at the pier. After he scooped up the bottle, he and Maggie walked down to where the dinghy was moored.

After they took the dinghy out to the research boat and came aboard, Zak briefed his team. A few minutes later, he and Maggie headed to the onboard lab. Zak slipped on a pair of white cotton gloves. Then he used a pair of small needle nose pliers to gently close around the blackened piece of tar or cork or God knew what that was stuck in the bottle's mouth. As he exerted just a bit of pressure, he twisted the pliers to the left.

Nothing.

He inhaled. Held it. Then he twisted the pliers the other way, while at the same time, he exhaled. But the stopper still didn't budge. He set the pliers down. Sighed.

Maggie leaned toward him and said, "So how old is it?" Her breath fanned his cheek. Zak felt warmth fill him. "Probably early-to-mid 1600s, judging from what I can see of the workmanship." He picked up the bottle and looked at its bottom and the edges where the bottom met the sides.

"There has to be a way to open the bottle," Maggie said.

He started to reach for the pliers again, but then he stopped. "You're right." He flashed her a smile as he rummaged around in a drawer until he found a rather battered pale green Bic lighter. After he shoved the drawer shut, he picked up the bottle in one hand and the lighter in the other. He angled the bottle so that it was almost

horizontal. He flicked the lighter and an orange-yellow flame burst from its top.

Maggie took a step backward. "Careful with that," she said.

"Yep." He positioned the lighter near the bottle's neck and slowly began to rotate it. The glass began to warm ever so slightly. A pungent, salty, sticky odor began to emanate from the tar or cork or whatever it was.

Maggie wrinkled her nose. "What *is* that?"

"Not really sure what they used to plug it," Zak said.

The glass warmed even more and he felt a bit light-headed from the stench. But he held the lighter with a steady hand and was rewarded with a faint *pop*. He reached up and gripped what was, he could now tell, clearly cork, between his thumb and index finger and slowly pulled upward. At first, the cork remained firmly in place. But as he continued to pull upward, the cork finally gave way with another little *pop*.

"What's inside?" Maggie said.

He angled the bottle so they could both look inside. Maggie put a hand on his arm as she leaned forward to peer in and his breath caught.

"Hmm. What's the best way to get that roll of paper out?" he murmured. Tweezers, he decided.

He took a pair from the drawer underneath the workbench and carefully fitted the tweezers into the bottle's neck. He clamped the tweezers onto the roll of yellowed, brownish paper and began to pull it out a millimeter at a time.

Maggie sucked in a breath. "Let's hope it doesn't crumble or tear."

Zak finally managed to free the rolled-up paper from its ancient prison. His heartbeat sped up as he glanced at Maggie. Her eyes sparkled as he held her gaze before he gently touched the age-darkened, curled page. As he uncurled the edges, pieces of the paper flaked off. Almost-black mottled spots sprinkled the brownish page at various intervals.

Zak winced and held his breath as the creased folds gave way. The paper lay in pieces instead of one full sheet. He focused on the faded cursive and, on an impulse, began to read it aloud.

Coastal waters off St. John's Island
12 July 1701   Henry Davies

Dearest Henry,

The time for our nuptials grows nigh. My heart soars like a bird a-wing. Oh, but for the taste of your kisses and the peace and joy that comes with our reunion. I fairly tremble with gladness to be soon in your arms. I have consulted the charts and believe we shall arrive on the shores of the fair St. John's Island two days hence.

Zak paused and glanced at Maggie. Longing tugged at his heart as she held his gaze for a moment longer than necessary. She cleared her throat and read the next passage.

Even as I write you, I have obtained a gown of finest silk. Though in truth, I should gladly stand by your side as wife in little more than rags if 'twould mean our togetherness sooner.

It gladdens my heart to know that your trading with the Mi'kmaq along the island's north shore Gulf has been so bountiful. I am gladder still that you have arrived unharmed from your voyages with that Company and are awaiting my missive thusly.

Maggie glanced at Zak and he saw an answering longing in her eyes, which was almost immediately replaced with an expectant look. So he took a breath to steady himself and read the final paragraphs, his heartbeat loud in his ears.

Mayhap I shall seal this within a bottle of the Caribbean's finest and, perhaps, toss it overboard? Nay, I jest. Though I have on more than one occasion, entertained such a fanciful notion.

Darling of my heart, though I do not wish to taint such a missive as this with disturbed news, I feel I must. My pendant has gone missing. I have little doubt who may have purloined it, though I shall wait to accuse him of thus until after our day of vow exchange three days hence. For nothing is as important as being with you once again.

Zak's voice grew husky and he stopped, unable to continue or to look up from the page. He blinked rapidly and exhaled in relief as Maggie's voice whispered the last lines.

Your affianced Beloved,
Eleanor

Zak rubbed his jaw and forced himself to look at Maggie. But she quickly averted her gaze and looked down at the desk top. "Zak, look. There's another scrap of paper here that was inside the bottle. With different writing scrawled on it."

Before Zak could respond, his grad assistant came into the room. "The sonar picked up three targets in this new location."

Maggie threw Zak a questioning glance. "Good news?"

Zak explained, "We've gleaned some new bits and pieces to go on after talking with locals, which have been helpful to triangulate a narrower search location. So we've used the sonar to scan the new area closer in to the bay."

"Oh?" Maggie said.

"The ship's sails were in flames, so there was no way to control it," Zak said. "So it would've probably drifted toward the rocks near the bay after it had been set ablaze."

Maggie glanced out the window then back at Zak. "Storm looks like it's holding off for now," she said. "You have to take this chance while you have it." She put a hand on Zak's arm. "You should go explore that first target here now."

Zak's eyes widened. Had Maggie seen he'd changed, after all? "Are...you sure about that? I know the pendant's important to you—"

"—and I know how important this is to you." She lifted her chin and crossed her arms.

Zak slowly turned back to his grad assistant. "Looks like it's something fairly large." He glanced at Maggie before he gave a nod to his assistant, "I want two others with me for the dive. We should bring down a lift bag, just in case whatever's down there is worth bringing to the surface."

ZAK GLANCED AT the elapsed time dial on his Hublot and then triple-checked his

oxygen. They'd been down here about fifteen minutes already.

He and the two other divers swam toward the large object submerged in the red silt on the sea floor.

As he swam toward it, he spotted several cannon balls strewn around.

The shape was oblong and a good size. He and his dive partners cleared away the excess sand and silt around the object.

He grinned. It looked like...a trunk?

As they continued to investigate, more cannon shot was revealed, along with musket balls, shards of china plates and silverware. Debris.

Zak's heart sped up. If this trunk was well preserved, what was inside just might provide vital clues about life aboard the ship and help him with the goals of this project.

That is, if it belonged to Eleanor's ship. But there was only one way to find that out. They'd have to bring it to the surface. The trunk rested on a gentle slope, sideways and at an angle to him.

They positioned the lift bag near the trunk. After some effort, they carefully extracted it then moved it into the bag. As Zak gave a last-minute check that everything was in order, he glanced back down at the now-exposed area where the trunk had been.

Was that...a ship's bell? His pulse pounded. If it was... He glanced at his Hublot. Not much air left. They had to get to the surface. He gestured to the other divers and they all began to swim upward.

Deck-side a little while later, Zak got out of his dry suit and into his T-shirt and jeans. He scrubbed a hand across his five o'clock shadow. He blew out an excited breath and headed over to the lab. "What do we have?"

"Looks like you were right. Some sort of trunk," his grad assistant said. "I'd say, judging from the construction, Spanish. Mid to late 1600s."

Zak took a step closer as he pulled on his white cotton gloves. "Let's go ahead and carefully take the top off before we start the conservation process."

The assistant nodded. "Wouldn't want to damage anything we might find inside."

The lock mechanism had seized up and must not have been locked when the ship went down because the lid creaked open in Zak's hands. His breath caught. Folded inside the trunk was a swath of material.

Aside from a few water stains, perfectly preserved.

Maggie gasped. "It looks like it was packed away yesterday."

Zak grinned. "It's because of the red clay substrate. The trunk was pretty much sealed inside the red clay undisturbed, which kept everything inside it preserved."

He closed his fingers around the material and lifted it out. A gown. He held it up. The style was definitely early 1700s. Which meant, this trunk very well could be from Eleanor's ship.

He cocked his head. It looked like—

"Silk," Maggie whispered. "This has to be Eleanor's wedding dress."

As Zak laid the dress down on the table, a single sheet of paper fell to the floor. It must have been tucked inside the dress's folds. He picked it up carefully. It was a logbook page.

H K F	Courses	Winds	Remarks: 15 July 1701
1 6 4	SSW	S.E.	1/2 past noon. We are in sight of coastal waters off Bay Fortune—62W longitude, 46N latitude. Storm clouds on horizon. —E.W.
2 6 5			
3 4 —	SSW		

4 5 — SSW off SW E

5 6 5	*WSW*	*N.E.*	*'Tis as I feared. Wind's shifted & weather has turned against us. The Quartermaster, too. His jealousy of my affections for H. has made him touched in the head. —E.W.*

6 4 6

7 3 —	*SW*	*N.N.E.*	*The wheel has been tied and my best men cut down. I have waited too long, been too sure of myself, to realize that I have spent all my efforts in trying to regain the pendant from the Quartermaster, when I should have solely concerned myself with returning to H. Though I fought the Quartermaster blade to blade, I cannot fight the blaze... 'Tis only a matter of time. I espy the lone dinghy and will make toward it though I think 'twill do no good now. I can only set this down and stow it in my trunk, with the hope that someday my words shall be read and this true account, if not consumed first by fire, be made known. —E.W.*

He stared down at the page. This lined everything up: the hour of the day, the speed of the ship in knots, what course they'd charted and the wind direction ... It clearly documented the last known location before Eleanor's ship went down. His pulse pounded. "With these additional points of reference on this logbook page, we can verify the site. Then use that to pinpoint the wreck area even more specifically. With allowances, of course, for time and tides."

Zak's grad assistant nodded. "I'll enter them into the computer and get the sonar to scan this specific region."

"Good. This trunk was Eleanor's, so it's more than likely that the mound of silt it rested on could conceal *Lady's Revenge*."

AFTER THE ASSISTANT left, and Maggie was alone with Zak, she said, "I've been looking at that scrap of paper while you were underwater. Might have something to do with the shipwreck." She pointed to the scrawled lines she'd noticed earlier.

Do not keep watch for the Highest light,
Where Fortune's fire no more burns bright.

Zak examined it. "It's rhyming." He looked at Maggie and murmured, "This might have something to do with the pendant, too."

"It's like the other riddles," she said.

Zak glanced back at the two lines, which, he noticed, had what looked like tiny squiggle marks underneath each line. "This looks like Davies' handwriting."

"So that means Davies must have gotten Eleanor's letter that was with this at some point," Zak mused.

"But did he receive Eleanor's letter in the bottle, or did he put the letter into the bottle?" Maggie asked.

"Either way, he must've put this extra note inside."

"Why would he do that?" Maggie frowned.

"I have no idea," Zak said. "But I suspect we may find out." He raised his eyebrows at her.

"Well, we're getting closer now," Maggie said. "We just have to figure out what it means."

"We *are* getting closer." His eyes flicked from the faded script back to Maggie's face.

Maggie's pulse jumped at the tone of Zak's voice. "So," she said hurriedly, "this is telling us *not* to keep watch for the highest light. What does that even mean?"

"Highest light...well, back 300 years ago, that could mean stars."

"Or a bonfire on a hill. Or cliff."

"Mmm." Zak repeated the first line. "Who would look for a light?"

"Sailors?" Maggie said.

"Wait a second. Do not keep watch... Keeping watch. What keeps watch?" Zak said.

"Watchtowers," Maggie guessed. "A lighthouse?"

Zak nodded. "But it's telling us not to keep a watch for lighthouses."

"So if we're not supposed to look for a lighthouse, what are we supposed to look for?"

"Look at the next line," he said. "For-tune with a capital *F*. I think it's referring to Bay Fortune, but it also mentions fire. Back then there was no lighthouse here. The British didn't even have the island yet. The French still did."

"So what could it mean?" Maggie asked.

"Well...the Vikings once explored this

area. When I was a student, I did a work study on that Viking site at L'Anse aux Meadows in Newfoundland. But I have a friend who found a rune stone here on P.E.I. And Bay Fortune is supposed to have had a Viking watchtower..."

"So I was right about the watchtower in that first guess." Maggie grinned at Zak.

"Funny how your first instincts are usually correct," Zak agreed.

Maggie caught his gaze but couldn't read his expression. Yet something had flashed in the depths of his gaze in the moments before he averted his eyes and looked back down at the page.

"Let's go," Maggie said.

JUST THEN, ZAK'S grad assistant poked her head around the door again. "Dr. Stuart? The sonar's ready." Zak looked at his assistant then back at Maggie.

Damn it.

This was not what he wanted to do. Choose between the wreck that could make his career, and the pendant that could make Maggie's.

Maggie bit her lip and glanced between him and his assistant.

If this were five days ago—hell, five hours ago—he might've let Maggie take her chances with the elements, the pendant.

But something in that look that had flashed between them only moments before, had his heart saying one thing, and his head another.

When would he get this opportunity again? This opportunity to uncover a wreck that had only existed before in legend... Or this opportunity to show Maggie what he truly thought, to make up for three years of not saying anything, not being supportive of her artistic career?

But this, this... would show her, with absolute clarity, what he should've told her long ago. That the history of someone else's life was not as important as the future of his own.

"Let's go," he said, as he headed to the door.

"But Zak." Maggie chewed on her bottom lip and put her hand on his arm. "If you go with me now, it won't help you find the shipwreck."

"It'll help you find the pendant."

"But I don't need the pendant any more," Maggie said. "I've gotten my inspiration now. So you don't *need* to do it."

"No," Zak said, "I don't need to do it—I want to do it. And that makes all the difference. So come on."

Maggie broke into a smile. "Can I just...?" She indicated a small clear plastic sleeve on the table. At Zak's nod, she tucked the extra piece of paper that had been inside the bottle, into the protective sleeve and then put the whole thing into her jeans pocket.

"Keep me posted. I shouldn't be gone too long," he said to his assistant as he and Maggie walked by on their way to the dinghy. "The moment you find anything more specific, call me."

"Sure thing," Zak's grad assistant said.

"But listen..." Zak scanned the horizon. "I know everyone's gung-ho, but if the storm ends up here, get yourselves ashore."

His assistant nodded, and turned back in the direction of the computers.

Zak picked the ancient bottle up off of the worktop. "Wouldn't hurt to bring this along since I didn't get a chance to look at it very closely yet," he said, as he tucked the bottle into an inner pocket of his windbreaker.

Then he and Maggie headed to shore and over to his pickup.

Rain began to fall.

Zak turned the radio on after he and Maggie jumped into the Dodge. *"Due to the rapid intensification of this storm in the last twenty-four hours, a hurricane watch is in effect for the Maritimes and specifically, Prince Edward Island. Record winds have begun to pound the south shore of the island near Borden-Carlton. The—"*

Zak changed the channel and glanced at Maggie. "Borden-Carlton's a ways from Bay Fortune here, but the storm's close."

"Well," she said, "that should keep the treasure hunters at bay, at least."

"Might make the cliffs around Bay Fortune especially dangerous. Even wash them away entirely."

"But we're too close to stop now," Maggie said.

Chapter Ten

THE RAIN LASHED against the windshield as Zak pulled onto a rutted red dirt track, and the wind flattened the acres of potato plants that grew in glossy green rows on either side of the road.

The truck rumbled further down the lane scored with dozens of recent tire tracks. "People have been here," Zak muttered. "This lighthouse is about the only historic landmark associated with Bay Fortune, so of course some of them would think to look here."

Maggie chewed her lip. "What if they found something?"

"Well," Zak said, "we don't really know what we're looking for, either, so I'd say everyone's on equal ground."

A stand of twisted and gnarled evergreens served as a buffer against the dramatic drop-off of these craggy cliffs along the South Shore.

And there, perched atop the highest, craggiest point, was the lighthouse. Zak leaned forward and looked up at it as the road dipped and wound its way toward what was left of the structure.

He glanced over at Maggie, raised his eyebrows then turned the radio to CBC.

"—*the Confederation Bridge has now been closed and a hurricane warning is in effect for all of P.E.I.—*"

Zak cut the engine.

"You sure this is the right place?" she said.

"Yes," Zak said. "They built this light-house in the 1800s. But what most people don't know is that the reason they built it here was because the foundation was the old Viking watchtower. The Vikings had already picked out a good spot and so the Scottish settlers—nothing if not practical—knew a good thing when they saw it. So they just used that foundation and made this lighthouse."

Black clouds boiled above the steel-gray surface of the Northumberland Strait. "You do realize this is kind of insane," Maggie said. But there was a gleam in her eyes.

"Just like that time we got caught in that nor'easter at Annapolis Royal, eh?" Zak said.

Maggie grinned.

Zak glanced out the windshield. "Storm's not that bad here. Yet." Almost as an afterthought, Zak grabbed the first aid kit. "We'll take shelter in the lighthouse if we need to. We'll be safe."

Maggie opened the passenger door as the rain began to pound harder. "Come on," Maggie said. "We'd better hurry or we might get washed away."

Zak got out too and zipped his jacket up just as the wind tried to rip it away from him.

"This way," he shouted over the gathering storm.

Maggie bent her head against a strong wind gust and followed Zak across a grassy field near the edge of the bay. The field was dotted with large and small holes. Shovels and picks lay scattered around, abandoned thanks to the storm. She moved ahead of Zak as they climbed up the narrow cliff-side path that led to the dilapidated lighthouse. Paint peeled off the clapboards. What had once been bright red around the door and window frames now had barely a hint of color.

The wind whipped Maggie's hair around her face as she increased her pace along the narrow path. As Zak hurried to catch up, the glass bottle banged against his ribs. Too bad there wasn't any rum left in it.

THE RAIN PELTED down harder. Another wind gust hit Zak in the chest. Just a little further and they'd be at the lighthouse door...

He kept one eye on the narrow path as the cliff fell away to his left. He glanced out at the water. The tide was coming in.

Ahead of him, Maggie slipped. Someone had dug a hole right next to the path. She scrambled to regain her feet on the crumbling, uneven ground but she stumbled, inches away from the sheer seven-foot drop off. Just as the wind gusted harder, she pitched forward. Zak lunged forward to snag the fabric of her shirt.

But he was too late.

His heart plunged as he watched her half-slide, half-tumble down the sheer bank. He sank to his knees by the cliff's edge. Pieces of earth broke away underneath his weight as he placed a palm against the cold ground and peered over the edge. His breath caught when he saw she wasn't moving. "Maggie!" he called. Zak's heart wrenched. How badly was she hurt?

But she looked up and grinned.

"I'm fine!" she yelled over the wind and rain. She stood and headed back toward the cliff face as the tide washed over her feet. The wind ripped at his hair and he could taste the saltwater in the air as she reached up toward him. She pointed to something just above her head then shouted something else, but the wind whipped her words away from him. He leaned even closer to the edge. Craned his neck so that he had a better view. His heart jumped as he realized what Maggie pointed at.

Tucked into a small crevice on the cliff face was a badly tarnished something that looked like it could have been, at one time,

a brass ring. Or a handle... on a treasure chest?

Maggie scrabbled up to a small ledge and grasped the weathered round brass handle with her free hand. Sea spray splashed against her legs.

Zak held his breath and watched as she tugged on the handle. It didn't move. Was it some sort of marker? Or part of a box?

"Maggie, you don't have time to do that!"

"Now is not a good time to start an argument with me, Zak," she yelled up at him between gritted teeth as she tugged on the ring again.

Bits of earth crumbled and fell away into the roiling waters below as she perched on the tiny outcropping that she'd somehow scrambled up onto. The tide rolled higher.

"I'm going to get you out of here," Zak called. He scooted forward on his stomach and stretched his hand down toward her. He could just brush her shoulder with his fingertips. "Can you move any higher?"

She shook her head.

Suddenly, a huge swell surged and Maggie's legs were submerged. The current sucked at her even as she gripped the ring.

As her grip tightened, more and more red earth crumbled away from her. Another surge swamped her lower body. It tugged at her as if she were a bathtub toy.

Zak, stretched out as far as possible, grasped a piece of her green T-shirt between his fingers at last and held on tight.

Another wave hit.

"You'll have to let go of the ring, Maggie! It's the only way."

"No!" She screamed over the roar of the waves and the lash of the wind. "What if it's the treasure chest?"

"Maggie!" he yelled back, "It's your life or a pile of gold. You have to let it go."

"I-I can't."

Was she crying?

A wave of empathy followed by frustration washed through him as yet another surge of water pummelled her. The force of the wave swept one of Maggie's legs out from under her.

And this time, she couldn't hold on to both the ledge and the ring. As the swell washed over Maggie, she let go and reached up to clasp Zak's arm.

"Damn it." He gritted his teeth and dug his toes into the earth but it did no good. He started to slide. She scrabbled for purchase but her other foot slipped off the ledge. He felt the full force of her body weight add to his as he lay on the bank.

"But I-I didn't get the chest," Maggie said.

Zak's heart lurched. He didn't care about any damn chest. Maggie's life was priceless. He wouldn't trade it for all the gold in the world. He reached down with his other arm and managed to grasp her other shoulder. Then leveraged himself around so that he could try to grip under her arms.

But he knew that he'd never be able to lift her up from this position.

He closed his eyes a second and a flash of those emerald-green eyes came to him. And...what was that sound? He cocked his head. He could've sworn he heard a voice that sounded like bluebirds and brooks in spring, whisper the words *pure hearted* in his ear under the keening of the wind. Yes. *This* was what Eleanor had meant. His eyes welled.

Just then, Maggie called, "I found another toehold! I think I can climb up."

Zak helped her heave herself over the edge of the cliff face. The wind and rain seemed to let up for a few precious moments as she scrambled, at last, to safety.

"God, Maggie." Zak's lips were on her hair, her cheeks, her forehead. "Are you *sure* you're all right?"

She nodded as her breath came in shallow gasps. He traced a finger down her cheek and under her chin. "Are you sure?" Concern filled his eyes.

Maggie sucked in a breath. Nodded. Then took another breath. "I'm okay," she managed then winced. "Besides the fact that my ankle hurts, I think I'm mostly fine." She staggered to her feet. "I had a realization while I was down there. That ring wasn't a box. It was some sort of ancient mooring stuck into the foundation. *Do not keep watch for the highest light...* We need to look at the bottom." She pointed to the foundation as she squinted against the onslaught of wind and rain.

Zak picked up the first aid kit. They reached the dilapidated doorway of the lighthouse as the wind began to howl and the rain turned needle-sharp.

A rusted padlock dangled from the door.

Hell. He didn't think to bring bolt cutters. Zak turned to jog back to his truck to get the pry bar and the toolbox from the bed. But Maggie grabbed his arm. She held up the lock—broken. She grinned and turned the knob. But it still wouldn't budge. He shouldered the door. But it was stuck fast. He felt Maggie shove against the door too.

At last, with their combined efforts, the old door finally gave way. The scent of musty air mixed with old lumber and a whiff of salt air, hit him as they stumbled inside.

MAGGIE FELT ZAK'S hand on her waist as she stumbled a few steps into the small space. She turned to look up at him. He met her gaze. But the shrill of his cell phone cut through the moment. He glanced at the device. "I have to take this. It's from my team."

He put the phone to his ear. Listened.

"We can't jump to conclusions." A pause. "Yes. Everyone's all right?" Another pause. "I'm fine. I'm with Maggie." More silence. Then, "I saw that. The bell had letters on it." He nodded. "You're sure? Right, yes. Wait for me to come and verify. We'll stay here til the storm passes. But I think we hit the jackpot." He hung up the phone.

"So," she said, "good news?"

"That debris trail actually led somewhere." He grinned. "The team's all safely ashore and they had time to analyze things. That sandy slope was part of *Lady's Revenge*. Turns out the silt covered the ship's bell—which confirmed it was *Lady's Revenge*."

"Really?" Maggie grinned back at Zak. "That's fantastic!"

Zak laughed. Maggie felt a tug in her chest. He sounded like the Zak she remembered.

"In really rare instances," he said, "in this case, with *Lady's Revenge*—if the silt can cover the wreck quickly enough, it preserves the wooden hull for thousands of years."

"And archaeologists like you live for things like that, don't you?"

Zak's grin widened. "But finding the wreck isn't the whole puzzle..."

"No." Maggie dragged her gaze from Zak and glanced around. "So where do we look now?"

"Under there could be a good place to look first." Zak pointed to a trap door. Maggie crouched down by it. Zak felt around the edges. Fit two fingers into a shallow depression and pulled upward. With a creak and groan, the door raised up on its hinges. Maggie peered over Zak's shoulder. Pitch black. He opened the first aid kit, pulled out a large flashlight and flicked it on. The powerful beam illuminated a series of crude steps carved into the sandstone bedrock that led down to a small hand-dug cellar.

"This had to be here in Davies' time," Zak murmured as his fingertips brushed the stone step. Maggie shivered as a sudden memory of Zak's fingers along her skin flashed through her mind. Zak lay the trapdoor down with a thud. He started down the steps and she followed. Damp sandstone and stale seawater stung her nose as he swung the light back and forth.

"What's that?" She pointed to a shape

in the darkest corner.

Zak trained the beam on it and moved toward the corner. "Looks like it's a pile of something...metal?" He nudged it with his boot and peered more closely. "From what I can tell, it was once iron bands. There's some pieces of wood clinging to the metal, too. So maybe it was a barrel? But it's pretty much nothing but rust and rotten wood splinters now." He turned to Maggie. "Can you hold the flashlight a sec?"

She took it from him, set it on the floor and aimed it at the low ceiling. The entire room was bathed in light.

"If my guess is right, those bands would've possibly been about the size and dimensions of a rum barrel—like would've been in here." He pulled out the old rum bottle from his inside pocket.

He idly turned it over in his hands and tapped the base against his palm. As he did so, his brow furrowed. "That's strange."

"What is?"

"The bottom of the bottle—it makes my hand look larger." His frown deepened as he held the bottle upside down, then looked down into the bottle after he turned it right side up again. "It works like a magnification device."

He held the bottle up to the light. "Yeah. It's like a primitive lens... I want to test out how strong the magnification is."

"Here." Maggie handed him the small piece that had been with Eleanor's letter. "This is the only piece of paper I have."

He examined the page through the bottle-lens. "Those squiggles are—"

"—more lines." Maggie's pulse raced.

Zak cleared his throat and read aloud.

For the heart
To finally be unbound,
ReTurn the treasured love
You have found.

"I assume *heart* means the pendant," Zak said, "so we have to *return the treasured love/you have found.*"

"But we haven't found any, uh, love, treasured or otherwise," Maggie said.

"And if we interpret it literally, that makes no sense," Zak added. "Not only that, it's impossible to return something we haven't found."

"Nothing is impossible," she said.

"Well..." Zak paused. "You know what I mean."

"Treasured love..." Maggie cocked her head. "Wait a sec. Eleanor received the gold from Kidd. In one of Eleanor's letters, she said she intended to give some of the gold to Davies for their life together..."

"So," Zak said, "maybe it literally means treasure."

"Right." Maggie's eyes grew round. "And the treasured love—maybe that means Eleanor gave her doubloons to Davies as a representation of her love for him."

"I thought that was the pendant."

"No. Remember the letters?" Maggie said. "She had the necklace long before she met Davies."

"Hmmm," Zak said.

"But," Maggie said, "doubloons..." She unzipped the interior pocket of her purse and pulled out the antique bracelet. "So your ancestor Samuel had gotten the coin and the pouch both from that innkeeper, Robert Morriss, who'd gotten both items from Beale. Beale got the doubloon and pouch from one of his treasure-hunting partners, John MacDonald, who was the grandson of Nicholas MacDonald. Nicholas, who must've passed on the coin to his grandson John, had served aboard *Lady's Revenge* under Eleanor. So Nicholas must have gotten the coin somehow from Eleanor. I bet she told him to give it to Davies. She did say in one of the letters that she trusted MacDonald completely."

"That's true," Zak said.

"Eleanor wanted the gold to be symbolic of her love for Davies."

"But it says *return*."

"And the *T* is capitalized." Maggie frowned again. Tapped a fingernail against her chin. "Well, maybe that's important. Maybe it's..."

"...also literal?" Zak raised his eyebrows at her.

"*Re-Turn*. Turn again. Turn what again though? I wonder if it means we're supposed to somehow turn the coin around?"

"But it's not attached to anything besides the chain," Zak pointed out.

Maggie sighed and fiddled with the coin on the bracelet.

"Turn can also mean twist. So maybe..." Zak looked at the bottle. Reached for the bracelet in Maggie's hand. "Can I...?"

Maggie held her breath as he picked up

the bracelet from her outstretched palm. "I just thought the edges of the coin were showing normal wear and tear since gold is soft," she said.

"But these irregular edges make it look like someone hacked away at it," Zak said. "So how does that connect with the other part...?" He nudged at the pile of iron dust and wood pieces with his boot. "There *was* a barrel sitting here. See how those pieces of wood are clinging to the last iron band? The wood is from the decayed barrel staves." He hefted the bottle in his hands.

"Which means, if there once were bands then *unbound* would fit."

"You're right. The iron bands of this barrel bound the wood together and held it all in place. So that means the treasure must have something to do with the barrel that was here."

He shone the flashlight down among the wreckage.

"Nothing there?" Maggie said.

Zak shook his head and sighed. "I mean, the trap door is right there in plain sight. Someone probably took whatever was down here years ago."

Maggie put a hand on his arm. "But we

have recovered some treasure of a sort."

Zak turned to her. "We *are* talking to each other again."

Maggie smiled. "Maybe that's what's important."

She glanced down at the now-exposed flagstone where Zak had brushed aside the pile of iron dust. "That's a funny indentation."

Zak looked where she pointed.

"That indent..." He swore under his breath and leaned closer to examine it. "It's carved out to look like the reverse of the head of a coin. This barrel wasn't put here by accident. Let me see the bracelet again."

Maggie handed it back to him. "It's a perfect fit," he murmured. He pressed the coin down hard into the crudely chiseled receptacle.

"Turn it," Maggie said suddenly. "We need to turn the coin." She glanced at Zak, a question in her eyes. He nodded.

She laid her fingers on top of his and they both turned the coin clockwise. There was a slight grating sound of stone on stone. The flagstone, which hadn't been mortared into place, shifted slightly to the side to reveal a small iron box.

Maggie caught her breath.

Zak glanced over at her. "You can do the honors."

The hinges stuck, but with Zak's help, the lid finally opened. The glint of gold winked back at them. Nestled in the middle of the pile of gold doubloons was a large emerald. It glowed softly in the dim light.

"The Pendant of the Pure Hearted," Zak said, as he looked into the chest.

"And these coins were Kidd's payment to Eleanor," Maggie added.

"Maybe you're right," Zak murmured as she caught him watching the expression on her face. She knew he didn't mean about the gold.

"I'm sorry," she said. "I've been such an idiot." A small smile appeared at her lips, and she looked up at him through her lashes. "I was lying to myself. About my designs. And about what my heart was telling me."

Maggie came closer to him. Placed a hand on his chest. For a moment, she said nothing and kept her eyes closed. She shook her head. She should've known it from the start. She'd just been trying to keep herself safe.

Fantasies didn't have flaws. Fantasies were safe. Safe and lonely. But she couldn't run to some fantasy. That was just in her head.

But Zak... Zak was here. Zak was warm and real and flesh and blood and he was here. Right here. In front of her.

She swallowed. She was in love with him. Flaws and all. "And Zak? I lied when I said I didn't love you." She moved her hand up to softly touched his cheek. "I'm sorry I said no to you. The truth is, I've never stopped loving you."

"It's okay." Zak shook his head. "I'm sorry for my behavior, too. I couldn't see past my anger. I couldn't see past your supposed betrayal of my trust. But I see now that we just weren't ready to move in the same direction."

Maggie drew in a jagged breath.

"But that's all in the past," Zak murmured.

For a moment, neither of them spoke.

Zak closed his eyes for a moment and whispered, "I've missed you." He opened his eyes, reached out, and laid a hand on her cheek. "So much."

He stroked a thumb down her cheek.

"Me too." She grazed her fingertips along his jawline.

Zak placed one hand over hers. Then reached down and picked up the pendant. The jewel glowed more, as if lit by an internal fire. His eyes briefly closed. When he opened them again and made eye contact with Maggie, she caught her breath at the tenderness in his gaze.

"Eleanor was right," Zak said simply and handed the pendant to her.

It felt warm and...almost alive in Maggie's cupped hands. It glowed even brighter and she felt an answering glow in her heart as she looked at Zak.

"So what are you going to do with that new jewelry design of yours?"

"Well," she said, "I've been thinking. I love designing and creating jewelry the most, and can do a lot of that from my laptop. I'll have more freedom, then. I thought about opening my own jewelry stores. But I've decided I can just be a jewelry supplier to local businesses—here and in New York." She smiled. "I think people are going to fall in love with my new design."

"Just like I'm falling in love with you?" Zak whispered. "Again."

The pounding of the rain on the roof and the lash of wind at the windows were drowned out by the rush of blood in Maggie's veins. "Yes." She laid her cheek against his shoulder. "Just like that. What about you?"

"Well, I'll be able to get the funding to mount a full-scale excavation of the wreck now that the triangulation was successful and we've found it. Not only that—" he grinned "—but I'll also be able to finish that final book chapter. Who knows? Maybe I'll even publish it myself. And now that you'll have more freedom, that means we can travel wherever we want. Together. We don't have to be stuck in different places."

"Yes," Maggie said. "I like that. A lot. So, I think it's time to head back."

Zak maneuvered the small iron box sideways and up and out of its hiding place. But as he did, the lid gapped open and the contents shifted slightly. "What's this?" He paused and picked up a sheaf of papers that lay underneath the gems and gold. One was a neatly folded piece of paper. The others were unfolded, with jagged edges along one side, as if they'd been torn from a book.

H—   Sept 5, 1701

Your plan pleased me greatly, as I, too, felt the burden of guilt from Eleanor's untimely death. As you know, I travelled to England in the first months of this year.

'Tis fortunate Kidd held Eleanor, you, and I, in such esteem, as I availed myself of the opportunity to pay a visit to him in Jail, so as to share with him our Knowledge. He gladly agreed to have me secret the coded message you directed, onto his Letter to the Speaker.

—N.M.

"A note from Nicholas to Davies," Maggie mused. "Which means, since Nicholas served as Eleanor's first mate, he must have been asked by Davies to write the third riddle," she said. "Then passed word on about it to his grandson John, who then must've told Beale..."

"Yeah," Zak said, "And then Beale wrote down the cipher key."

"But if Eleanor intended the gold for Davies, why was he writing clues to hide it?" Maggie asked.

"Hmm," Zak said, "Maybe he couldn't bear to keep it with him, but didn't want to part with it, either?" They turned their attention back to the uncovered pages.

2 June 1701

Kidd is dead. Eleanor would have been a-grieved, had she known of it. Though I wonder, some nights, if she somehow does...

Maggie read the next entry over Zak's shoulder.

16 July 1701

She is dead. I have wrestled her beloved necklace from the grasp of the Quartermaster, Kidd's former crewman—James Fitzhugh. The gold, as well. Though I longed to drive a blade through his heart for what he has done, I have withheld such urgings. Instead, I trust to Fate that his end shall not be a Pleasant one, to atone for those Sins he has committed.

"So the gold Kidd had given Eleanor had ended up with Davies," Maggie murmured and then continued to read.

22 July 1701

Lately I feel Eleanor's presence, as if she is urging me to do something, though I know not what that may be. I have begun to salvage what is of use that has washed inland from Lady's Revenge.

I have decided I shall stay here amid the Mi'kmaq on this Isle cradled on the waves. 'Tis become my home. Though I could not share it with Eleanor, I do continue to feel her presence. It comforts me greatly.

30 Oct 1701

At last I believe I know what Eleanor has been urging. So, I have taken precautions. I've safely hidden the pendant I retrieved from the Quartermaster, along with the rest of the doubloons and other gems that I gathered from Lady's Revenge when they washed into some shallows.

'Tis all that's left of her worldly

possessions. And that which was freely given her by that Indian wise woman and Kidd. Though it grieves me some, as that treasure trove she and I originally conceived of as the means to our happy life together.

16 April 1702

I have sought and found a way to honor my Beloved, and the memory of our Love. I have written up two riddles, as a testament to our love, our saga. May there be a way for those with strong constitutions—as my Eleanor had; and with pure-hearted love—as our union was to be—to solve the verses.

Whoever so does shall be thusly rewarded with the treasure that I have aforementioned, should they take the time to be diligent and thorough in their quest. After I received Eleanor's letter of 12 July, I decided to place it inside an empty bottle of the Caribbean's finest, as Eleanor had made reference to. I hid one of the riddles inside the bottle, as well. I have also secreted the treasure. I do believe this is what she would have wanted, and I do it solely to honor her memory, to honor our Love. May she rest in peace.

"So these are the missing pages from Davies' journal," Zak said, as he replaced all the papers, closed the lid and tucked the box under his arm.

He took Maggie's hand and went up the cellar stairs, across the scarred wooden floor of the lighthouse, and outside. The clouds began to soften to a dove gray. "Looks like the storm is ebbing." He reached up to stroke Maggie's hair.

Maggie looked up at Zak and smiled. But then she gasped. Pointed out into the harbor. Zak turned to look. Off in the distance, the clouds parted to reveal a rainbow arched across the sky. Underneath the rainbow, white sails billowed in the non-existent breeze. Red, yellow, green and white signal flags flapped all along the mainsail.

A stately four-masted tall ship sailed around the end of the point and disappeared.

"Looks like we broke the curse," Mag-

gie whispered.

Zak reached for her hand and intertwined his fingers with hers. "No curse," he said softly, and looked toward the end of the point. "Just everlasting joy for what was, and now shall always be." He turned his gaze back to her and smiled. "We've found not only the treasure, but also each other." He ran a hand along her cheek and whispered, "And now, it's for always." Zak leaned in and kissed her.

Thanks for reading! Want more treasure hunting and romance?

If you enjoyed *Now It's For Always*, then don't miss Nicky's story in *At Last It's True Love.*

It's the third title in the Prince Edward Island Love Letters & Legends trilogy.

Visit www.jessicaeissfeldt.com to find out more!

Acknowledgments

Karen Dale Harris—developmental editor, whose excellent insights and suggestions helped me shape this story into its final form

My parents, Sabrina Volman and J. Esmee McAskill—beta readers, who were awesome and read and encouraged this story from manuscript to publication

Jane Dixon-Smith—graphic designer, who gave me a beautiful cover for the story

Kirsten M. Hawley—underwater archaeologist, who very kindly and patiently answered my numerous questions and read through relevant parts of the narrative for archaeological, technical and scientific accuracy

Author's Note

I've always loved the movies *National Treasure* and *Pirates of the Caribbean*. So when I learned about the sightings of the Ghost Ship of the Northumberland Strait on P.E.I., I knew I had the kernel of an idea for the second book in this series, and just *had* to do something to combine romance, treasure hunting, and ghostly ships!

When I wrote this novel, I wanted to be as accurate as possible, and as true-to-reality as the facts would allow. However, there were instances when, because of the time periods of this book, it wasn't possible. So I took artistic license to modify dates, timelines, and such to fit the storyline. For example, the first documented sightings of the ghost ship are really in 1786, not in 1701, as I've written in this novel. (Though perhaps the early P.E.I. settlers did see it but didn't bother to write about it?) Memorial University does indeed have an archaeology department but they don't actually have a nautical archaeology program—I took the liberty of inventing that position for Zak.

When I researched Dalvay and its original owner, Alexander MacDonald, I wasn't able to uncover anything about his ancestors. So I took artistic license and gave him ancestors who sailed with Captain Kidd.

I also made a few timeline tweaks to *The Prince Edward Island Magazine, Volume I*. It was actually published in 1899, but, for the sake of this story's timeline, I've modified its publication date to be 1848.

The Viking settlement in Newfound is real. But the P.E.I. Viking watchtower and Bay Fortune-area lighthouse are purely figments of my imagination, as is the craggy cliff I've placed the fictitious lighthouse atop. And, while there are cliffs along the South Shore, there aren't any around the Bay Fortune area.

The Beale Papers truly exist, but have no ties (that I know of!) to P.E.I.

And remember, if you decide to drive the shoreline of Prince Edward Island, keep your eyes open for the ghostly tall ship... You just might see it!